Colaba
Nights

Shiv Bhowmik

NewDelhi • London

BLUEROSE PUBLISHERS
India | U.K.

Copyright © Shiv Bhowmik 2025

All rights reserved by author. No part of this publication may be reproduced, stored in a retrieval system or transmitted in any form or by any means, electronic, mechanical, photocopying, recording or otherwise, without the prior permission of the author. Although every precaution has been taken to verify the accuracy of the information contained herein, the publisher assumes no responsibility for any errors or omissions. No liability is assumed for damages that may result from the use of information contained within.

BlueRose Publishers takes no responsibility for any damages, losses, or liabilities that may arise from the use or misuse of the information, products, or services provided in this publication.

For permissions requests or inquiries regarding this publication, please contact:

BLUEROSE PUBLISHERS
www.BlueRoseONE.com
info@bluerosepublishers.com
+91 8882 898 898
+4407342408967

ISBN: 978-93-7139-942-5

Cover design: Yash Singhal
Typesetting: Namrata Saini

First Edition: June 2025

Dedication

To Maa and Baba—
who held me when the world let go,
who heard the words I never said,
and believed in me even when I forgot how to.

You've been the quiet strength behind every broken moment,
the hands that lifted me—again and again—
without complaint, without pause.

In your love, I found my footing.
In your patience, I found my voice.
And in your unwavering faith,
I found the courage to write this story.

This book breathes because of you.

With all my heart,
—Shiv

Overview

Vaani & Aakash – Colaba Nights is a poetic, emotionally rich novel chronicling the story of Vaani and Aakash, two young souls who collide in the old-world charm of Colaba, Mumbai. Their journey unfolds from innocent sparks to deep intimacy, unspoken heartbreaks, and the painful beauty of letting go. Set against the vibrant yet fading backdrop of a city that never sleeps, their love story lingers beyond time, leaving behind questions, grief, and a legacy of words.

Contents

Prologue *1*

Chapter One: The First Spill 4

Chapter Two: Windowed Smiles and Scarlet Letters 12

Chapter Three: Of Fireflies and Firsts 22

Chapter Four: Rain Between the Lines 30

Chapter Five: Cracks in the Calm 41

Chapter Six: Distance in the Silence 47

Chapter Seven: Her Own Shadow 57

Chapter Eight: The Arrival of Reyan 67

Chapter Nine: Fractures and Falsettos 78

Chapter Ten: Between Two Fires 90

Chapter Eleven: Quiet Spaces, Quieter Hearts 101

Chapter Twelve: When the Lights Flickered 108

Chapter Thirteen: Salt and Flame 114

Chapter Fourteen: After the Burn 119

Chapter Fifteen: A Quiet Return 124

Chapter Sixteen: The Echo of Almost 129

Chapter Seventeen: What the Night Unfolds 136

Chapter Eighteen: The Door That Waited 141

Chapter Nineteen: The Shape of Something Real 146

Chapter Twenty: The Letter in the Mailbox 150

Chapter Twenty-One: The Last Night 155

Chapter Twenty-Two: The Departure 160

Chapter Twenty-Three: The Strangers We
Almost Loved 166

Chapter Twenty-Four: What We Thought We'd Hold. 171

Chapter Twenty-Five: Letting the Thread Go 176

Chapter Twenty-Six: The Versions We Become 180

Chapter Twenty-Seven: The Crossing 185

Chapter Twenty-Eight: The Lingering 189

Chapter Twenty-Nine: All That Followed 193

Chapter Thirty: The Storm We Didn't See Coming 197

Chapter Thirty-One: The Morning After the
Goodbye.. 202

Chapter Thirty-Two: The Last Song............................... 206

Chapter Thirty-Three: In the Wake of Silence.............. 211

Author Introduction.. *216*

Acknowledgments.. *217*

Preface *218*

Foreword.. *219*

Prologue

Colaba never forgets.

Not the scent of salt drifting through its winding lanes, nor the scratchy melodies leaking from old vinyl players in antique cafés.

Not the faded signs above crumbling bookstores, or the way the Arabian Sea breathes against the stone promenade—tired, eternal, forgiving.

And certainly not the kind of love that once bloomed quietly between cracked bookstore shelves and over steaming cups of roadside chai, as the ocean whispered secrets only two hearts could ever hope to understand.

This is the story of Vaani and Aakash.

She was a writer of unspoken things—words she never said aloud, emotions she stitched between sentences.

He was a musician who tucked his grief between chords, letting melodies carry the ache he never named.

They met by accident—an upturned cup of tea on a rainy evening, a clumsy apology, a hesitant smile.

What began as playful glances and cinnamon-scented conversations soon deepened into something far more intricate:

A love without a script.

A love without a clock.

A love that lived not in declarations but in quiet, stubborn persistence.

But timing is a silent villain.

And so are the walls we build when we're too afraid to ask for more.

What follows is a journey written in the language of longing—

of distance measured in unspoken words,

of devotion stretched thin by missed calls and misplaced pride,

of midnight walks haunted by the memory of someone who was almost enough.

Through seasons of almosts and almost-endings, through strangers who felt like poor imitations, they learned that sometimes, love doesn't vanish.

It just... changes shape.

It folds itself quietly into the corners of your life, pretending not to matter, while reshaping everything you are.

Colaba Nights isn't merely a romance.

It's an elegy—to the ones we lost even while they were still breathing beside us.

It's a love letter to all the almosts.

A hymn for the grief that lingers longer than the memory of the last kiss.

It's about art. And ache.

About becoming the person love once dared you to be—

even after love is gone.

Because when love dies, it doesn't always go quietly.

Sometimes...

it sings.

And sometimes, if you're lucky,

it leaves behind one last song.

Chapter One

The First Spill

The night had wrapped Colaba in a velvet kind of warmth, dipped in honey and dusted with salt. It was the kind of evening that didn't make the news, didn't shake the earth, and didn't change history. But it lingered—like the scent of something sweet just after it leaves the room.

The roads were damp from an afternoon drizzle that had come and gone like a passing mood. Streetlamps flickered gold on the slick tar, casting dreamy halos that stretched like yawns. The sea was close by, audible if you paid attention—a slow exhale of waves against the old stone barricades of Marine Drive, like the city's heart beating in hushes.

Rickshaws rattled. Vendors sold bhutta charred to perfection. The air smelled of salt, damp newspapers, and roasted peanuts in newspaper cones. A violinist stood near the Gateway, his fingers coaxing out a tune that sounded too soft for such a loud city. Still, it stayed afloat— melancholic, thin, sweet. A kind of music that found you if your heart was cracked enough to let it in.

And it found her.

Vaani walked with her head tilted slightly upward, as if she were waiting for the sky to speak to her. Or maybe she was just watching the clouds bruise into twilight. Her canvas tote bag hung heavy on her shoulder, overstuffed with a mess of library notes, ink-streaked textbooks, and that same tattered copy of *The Unbearable Lightness of Being* she always carried, even though she'd read it so many times that the spine barely held anymore.

She had just stepped out of St. Xavier's, where she'd spent hours buried in dusty shelves, breathing in the strange quiet of old pages and older pain. She'd been reading about Partition again—letters from refugee camps, songs stitched with grief, poems left unfinished because the poets never made it to safety. There was something about the silence in libraries that made her feel less alone, but the weight of history always followed her out like a shadow.

In her hand, she clutched her small comfort—a paper cup of cinnamon-spiced chai from the Irani stall near the university gates. She drank it almost religiously. Sweet. Sharp. Familiar. She took small sips, like she was afraid it might disappear too soon.

She was tired. Not the kind of tired that a nap could cure. The kind that made her bones ache and her thoughts loop. She hadn't replied to her best friend's text. She hadn't called her mother back. She hadn't eaten anything since noon except a samosa she didn't even remember chewing.

And she was thinking of a dream again—the recurring one, where she ran barefoot down a beach she couldn't name, chased by a tide that always stopped just short of catching her. And that Leonard Cohen line played in her mind like a scratched record: *"Love is not a victory march, it's a cold and broken hallelujah."*

Which is why she didn't see him.

Not until it was far too late.

She collided into him like a sentence tripping over its own punctuation.

Hot chai sloshed upward in slow motion. The cup spun out of her hand like a tiny, caffeinated UFO. The notebook slipped from her tote and landed on the pavement with a resigned flop. The pen followed with a clink that barely registered against the sudden rush of her panic.

"Oh God!" she gasped. "Oh no, no, no—"

The man, wearing a crisp white shirt that now bore a large, spreading stain the color of sunset, blinked at her.

Just blinked. As if someone had pressed pause.

Vaani froze.

So did time.

The city didn't. A scooter honked behind them. A paan-stained man on the corner called out for change. But in the little circle of shame she had just created, there was only cinnamon-scented disaster and a stranger soaked in it.

She opened her mouth. Then closed it.

Then opened it again. "I'm—I'm so sorry! I wasn't looking—I didn't see you—I mean, obviously—but—oh God, your shirt—"

The stranger looked down at the spill, then back up at her. And slowly—very slowly—one eyebrow arched. Then came a smirk.

A maddening, lopsided, deliberately unbothered smirk.

"Well," he said, his voice smooth, calm, and entirely too amused for someone freshly baptised in chai. "If this is how you welcome neighbors, I'm very intrigued."

Vaani stared. "Neighbors?"

He nodded. "Just moved in. White bungalow, three houses down. And apparently right into the splash zone."

She wanted the footpath to swallow her whole. Or the sky to rain down a bolt of lightning. She had made her peace with embarrassment before—but this was... this was something else.

"I can pay for dry cleaning," she blurted. "Or buy you a new shirt. Or—"

He chuckled. It was low and warm, the kind of laugh that didn't mock you but invited you to join in the ridiculousness of it all.

"Relax. I've had worse first impressions. None of them smelled this good, though."

She blinked. "It's cinnamon. From the Irani stall."

"Your comfort drink?"

She nodded. "More like emotional life support."

"I get that." He bent down, picked up her fallen notebook, tapped the dust off with deliberate care, and handed it to her.

Their fingers brushed.

Only briefly. But enough to send a little ripple through her chest.

He knelt and retrieved her pen too, as if this were a perfectly rehearsed act of chivalry.

"Here. Would hate to see a girl lose her words."

She took both items back and tucked them into her bag, heart still thudding louder than necessary.

"I'm Aakash," he said, sticking out his hand.

She hesitated only for a second. "Vaani."

Their handshake was short but steady.

"So, History major?" he asked, eyeing the title on her notebook.

"Yep," she said. "With a minor in masochism."

Aakash laughed again, that easy, disarming sound. "I write music," he offered. "Mostly lyrics. Some instrumental stuff when the muse isn't being a diva."

"Oh," she said, suddenly interested. "Professionally?"

"Dreamingly," he corrected.

They stood awkwardly in the moment. The streetlight above them flickered, casting a soft yellow glow that made everything feel like a stage set too perfectly for coincidence.

"Well," he said, breaking the pause, "if you're not planning to throw another drink at me, mind if I walk with you?"

Vaani gave a small, reluctant smile. "Only if you promise not to report me to the Chai Council."

"No promises," he said, falling into step beside her.

They walked in silence for a few seconds.

The kind of silence that wasn't heavy. Just unhurried.

Bougainvillea vines draped over compound walls like gossip. The soft thrum of distant music bled into the evening. Somewhere, a couple argued softly over what to eat for dinner.

"So," Aakash said, "what else does Vaani do when she's not assaulting strangers with tea?"

"I write too," she admitted. "Not music. Just… things. Snippets. Half-poems. Journal entries I never finish."

"That's still writing."

She shrugged. "It's mostly private. Like thoughts you don't want to leave your head but also don't want to keep."

He nodded like he understood. "And gaming?"

She glanced at him sideways. "Stalker?"

"Educated guess. You've got the introvert-slash-imaginary-worlds vibe."

She laughed. "Fair. I do game. It helps quiet the noise."

Aakash turned his head slightly to look at her. "You're… kind of a unicorn."

"Please don't say that."

"I meant it in the least cheesy way possible."

"There's no way to say that without cheese."

"I stand corrected. You're a cynical unicorn."

She laughed louder this time. It startled even her.

They slowed near a corner where the trees parted enough for the moon to spill onto the pavement like cream.

"Favorite book?" he asked.

"Don't make me choose."

"Fine. Desert island book."

She pretended to think. "Something by Murakami. Or maybe... Neruda's poems. Depends on whether I'm escaping or healing."

He nodded approvingly. "And song?"

"You first."

"Right now?" he paused. "'The Night We Met' by Lord Huron."

Vaani smiled. "Good choice. Very... midnight heartbreak vibes."

"Exactly."

By the time they reached her building, it felt like no time had passed and also like they'd known each other for years.

"This is me," she said, stopping at the base of the stairs.

He pointed across the narrow lane. "That's mine."

Her eyes widened. "No way."

"Destiny," he said. "And a chai-stained shirt."

They both laughed.

There was a beat. A pause filled with possibility.

"I guess this is goodnight," she said.

"Only if you want it to be."

"I do," she said, quietly. "But maybe not goodbye."

"Deal."

She climbed two steps, turned back. He was still standing there, hands in his pockets, eyes steady.

And just like that—under a bruised sky, with nothing more than a paper cup, a quiet walk, and a ruined shirt between them—

a story began.

Chapter Two

Windowed Smiles and Scarlet Letters

The next morning carried the perfume of wet earth and the muted soundtrack of a city waking up slowly. A pressure cooker hissed three floors above, accompanied by the clang of vessels being rinsed somewhere nearby. A radio played a grainy old Lata Mangeshkar tune, her voice gliding like a memory through the walls. Pigeons warbled from their makeshift balconies, and the ceiling fan overhead hummed in lazy spirals. Mumbai, on a monsoon morning, wasn't loud. It was layered. Like someone had peeled back the chaos to reveal a heartbeat.

Vaani sat cross-legged on her tiny porch swing, wrapped in an oversized cardigan that had long forgotten its original owner—her sister's, she thought, maybe stolen, maybe borrowed. It had holes in one sleeve and threads dangling from the hem, but it felt like home. Her hair, still damp from her shower, curled at the nape of her neck in little wisps. In her hands rested a ceramic mug that steamed upward, the scent of masala chai rising like a quiet prayer. Today, she'd swapped her usual cinnamon brew for something stronger, more grounding. Her heart wasn't asking for comfort—it was asking for clarity.

On her lap lay *The Scarlet Letter*, dog-eared and underlined, a highlighter tucked between pages that hadn't been read in earnest. The yellow ink had bled through some lines, but Vaani didn't mind. She liked her books messy. Annotated. Lived in.

Her eyes, however, weren't on the text. They drifted between words and thoughts, mostly toward last night—toward the splash of chai, the arc of a paper cup midair, and the crooked smile of a stranger who made the city tilt ever so slightly. Aakash. His name felt strange on her tongue. Not heavy. Just new.

"In the books again?" a voice called out, and her daydream split clean in the middle.

She looked up, blinking through pale sunlight and the ghost of that memory.

Aakash stood just beyond her gate, fresh from a morning run. His hair was damp, curling slightly at the edges, and his black t-shirt clung to his torso in all the ways her brain wasn't ready to process before caffeine. He leaned against the gate casually, like it belonged to him. Like he belonged there.

Vaani tried—failed—to act unfazed. "Kinda hard not to when I've got seventy pages of guilt, sin, and 17th-century misogyny waiting for me."

He chuckled, stepping forward. "Scarlet Letter, huh?"

She nodded, lifting the book slightly like it weighed more than it did. "Nothing like public shaming and repressed Puritans to really kick off the weekend."

His laughter came easily, the kind that lived in the chest before spilling out. "Sounds like my last relationship."

She raised an eyebrow. "That bad?"

He wiped a bead of sweat from his brow using the hem of his shirt. The motion exposed a flash of skin before fabric fell back into place. Vaani pretended not to notice. "Not unless you're a walking metaphor for guilt and societal hypocrisy," he teased.

She grinned, shaking her head. "You're impossible."

"Guilty," he said with a half-bow. "Anyway, I should finish this run before I convince myself that buttered toast is a better idea than cardio."

She sipped her tea, buying time to calm her heartbeat. "See you later?"

He nodded, gaze holding hers just a breath longer than necessary. "Count on it."

She watched him jog away, each footfall quiet against the puddled street. When he turned the corner, she looked down at her book again but didn't read. The words blurred. Hester Prynne faded. All she saw was that smile.

The rest of the morning passed slowly, like honey dripping from a spoon. Vaani lingered on her swing a little longer, tracing the rim of her mug with her thumb, the book still open on her lap but long forgotten. Occasionally, her gaze would drift toward the narrow street, half-expecting another glimpse of Aakash running back, or maybe just waving from his balcony.

Silly, she told herself. But the kind of silly that made her toes curl slightly into the soft mat below.

By noon, the sky had turned an irritable gray—typical of July afternoons in Mumbai—ready to burst into a downpour at the slightest provocation. But the rain held back, like a story waiting for the right line.

Vaani spent the early part of her day half-studying, half-procrastinating. The Scarlet Letter lay on her desk, highlighter untouched. Instead, she found herself scribbling into her notebook—fragments of poems she didn't intend to finish, phrases like "breaths borrowed from strangers" and "kisses made of vanilla and dare." Even when she paused to do the dishes or tie up her hair, her mind kept circling the same orbit: the chai incident, the porch smile, and the not-quite-accidental way he said, *"Count on it."*

It was sometime after four when she saw him again— through the slats of her window, half-obscured by the bougainvillea vine curling around her balcony grill.

He was shirtless now.

Not in a calculated, posing-for-attention way. Just in a lazy, it's-too-humid-for-fabric sort of way. His bare chest glistened faintly, catching the light as he lounged on a jute mat laid across his balcony floor. A battered guitar sat on his lap, his fingers moving over the strings in slow, deliberate strokes. His head was tilted back, eyes closed, one foot tapping lightly to an unheard rhythm.

Vaani held her breath.

She knew she should look away. That it was impolite. Creepy, even. But she didn't. Couldn't. There was something about that quiet—him, the city, the stillness of monsoon air—that felt like watching a secret. Not meant for her, maybe. But not entirely forbidden either.

And then—just for a heartbeat—he opened his eyes and looked straight at her window.

Vaani froze.

He didn't wave. Didn't smirk. Just held her gaze for half a second longer than comfort allowed. Then went back to his guitar.

She closed the curtain with a sudden rush of embarrassment and pressed her back against the wall, heart pounding like she'd just sprinted up five floors.

God. What was she doing?

By the time evening approached, the city had changed outfits again. From overcast gray to a bruised lavender. The clouds—heavy with secrets—stretched across the sky like spilt ink. They didn't weep, not yet. But they threatened to. That restless kind of monsoon weather that made every street corner feel like it was holding its breath.

Vaani stood in front of her mirror, turning sideways, then back again. She wasn't dressed up—just jeans and a navy blue top that hugged her frame gently, nothing dramatic. A hint of rose oil on her wrists. Kajal smudged under her eyes. She looked... familiar. But more alert. As if something inside her had tilted, just a little, since last night.

"Ready or not," she whispered to herself, pulling open the door.

Aakash opened his within seconds, towel still slung around his neck, droplets clinging to his curls like they didn't want to leave. He grinned the second he saw her.

"What's up, schoolgirl?" he teased, eyes flicking briefly to her book-free hands.

She raised an eyebrow. "Thought I'd take a break from shame-soaked Puritan Boston and see how the cool kids live."

"Risky choice," he said, stepping back. "Give me five to become a functioning human being. Then I'm all yours."

She tried to say something clever, but her stomach flipped spectacularly, drowning any chance of it.

When he returned, now in a soft grey tee and ripped jeans, they fell into step naturally. Their pace was slow, unhurried, like the city itself. Colaba looked different in golden hour—everything was dipped in syrupy light. Even the peeling paint on the buildings looked poetic. Pastel pinks. Washed-out blues. Moss-streaked corners. Bougainvillea vines curling like lazy secrets across windowsills.

They didn't talk much at first. Their shoulders brushed once. Then again. And neither stepped away.

"There's this place near Regal," Vaani said after a while, hands in her back pockets. "They do milkshakes that are better than heartbreak therapy."

Aakash turned to her, intrigued. "Better than therapy? Bold claim."

"Life-changing," she promised.

When they reached the stall—a blink-and-miss hole in the wall wrapped in fairy lights and peeling blue paint—he whistled.

"You undersold it."

The scent of vanilla, frying oil, and powdered chocolate hung heavy in the air. The benches out front were faded pink and sky blue, mismatched and chipped, but charming.

They sat side by side, sipping thick vanilla milkshakes from old-fashioned steel tumblers, their fingers occasionally brushing as they passed each other the fries. The air between them grew easier with each laugh, each shared story, like the rhythm of an inside joke forming in real time.

"I write lyrics," Aakash said, tapping out rhythms on the bench's armrest. "Sometimes they become songs. Other times, just scattered words I leave in voice notes and forget."

"That's kind of beautiful," Vaani said, stirring her straw. "Like thoughts that don't need to be judged to be worthy."

"And you?"

"I write things," she confessed. "Scraps. Notebooks full of half-formed feelings. Stuff I'm too scared to show anyone."

He leaned in, eyes gentle. "Ugly's good. Ugly means it's yours."

She flushed, surprised at how that settled into her chest like permission.

"You're surprisingly poetic for a guy who got doused in chai less than twenty-four hours ago."

"And you're surprisingly brave for someone who's got ketchup on her lip," he said with a grin.

She froze, reaching up in horror.

He beat her to it. Reached over and wiped it gently with his thumb.

Her breath hitched. His touch wasn't flirty. It wasn't possessive. It was soft. Careful. Like he knew exactly how much to give and when to stop.

"There," he murmured.

The air shifted.

It wasn't loud, the way feelings often are. It was quiet—like breath drawn between notes in a song. But it changed everything.

"You're trouble," she whispered, half-smiling.

He didn't deny it.

Later, they wandered toward the sea.

The streets were quieter now, softened by dusk. Street vendors lit small kerosene lanterns, their stalls flickering with shadows and warmth. A child ran past them with a toy windmill that spun furiously in the wind, laughter trailing behind him like ribbon.

The pier welcomed them like an old friend—weathered, wooden, and waiting. It stretched into the Arabian Sea like a promise half-kept. The swing set nearby creaked gently in the breeze, its chains rusted, its seat faded, but still hanging on.

They sat side by side, their knees brushing, sneakers gently tapping the dusty ground beneath. The ocean's breath rose to meet them, salt-kissed and tired. Above, the sky had turned ink-blue, a few stars brave enough to peek out from behind clouds.

Vaani toyed with the frayed rope of her swing, her fingers tracing the knots like they held answers.

"I want to do something reckless," she said suddenly, as if the thought had leapt out before she could tame it.

Aakash turned, the curiosity in his eyes soft, not invasive. "Define reckless."

She looked straight ahead, into the sea, then back at him. "I want to kiss you."

The words hung there. Undressed. Vulnerable. True.

He didn't laugh. Didn't smirk.

He stilled.

The swing rocked once beneath them, a breath between decisions.

"Are you sure?" he asked, his voice quieter than the waves.

She nodded, her chest tight with hope and terror. "If I don't, I'll regret it."

And then—like exhaling into a question—he smiled. The kind of smile that made you forget what came before it.

"Then don't regret it," he whispered.

He leaned in first. Or maybe she did. Later, neither of them would remember who closed the distance.

Their lips met—tentative, then certain. A hush between two heartbeats. The kiss was gentle at first, like a hello. Like finding the first line of a poem after months of silence. Then it deepened, slow and full of trembling wonder. His hand found her waist, not demanding, just present. Her fingers curled into the fabric of his shirt.

She tasted vanilla and salt and something new. Something beginning.

When they pulled apart, breathless but not startled, he rested his forehead against hers.

"You responded," she said softly, her voice caught between laughter and disbelief.

"Was I not supposed to?" he murmured, eyes still closed.

"I didn't expect it."

"I didn't either," he admitted. "But I couldn't not."

She smiled then—a soft, secret smile meant only for him. "Perfectly reckless," she whispered.

He kissed her again, slower this time. Deeper. Like punctuation. Like a promise.

And for a while, they just sat there. Swinging gently. The sea humming beneath them. The sky bearing witness to a beginning neither of them had planned for, but both suddenly needed.

When they finally stood and walked back through the lanes of Colaba—lit now with warm window lamps and soft music bleeding through half-closed shutters—their hands found each other's. Not by accident. Not shyly.

On purpose.

Their fingers laced like they'd always meant to.

A page had turned.

And somewhere between spilled chai, vanilla shakes, and a kiss by the sea—a new story, their story—had begun.

Chapter Three

Of Fireflies and Firsts

The next few days passed like slow-burning verses of a love song—unhurried, humming beneath the din of the city. Colaba had not changed, not really. The same cracked footpaths, the same honking rickshaws, the same scent of sea and spice. But to Vaani, it had been rewritten.

Each corner was now punctuated with memory: a laugh shared near the tea stall, the shape of Aakash's silhouette through the slats of her balcony curtain, the echo of his guitar faintly bleeding through concrete walls.

They had crossed from strangers to something else—something more intricate than friendship but still suspended just shy of definition. Their meetings weren't planned. They simply happened. A shared morning glance from balcony to balcony. A knock during dusk with no reason at all. A gentle nod outside the grocery store, followed by a smirk and a shrug.

It was Tuesday evening when he knocked again.

No warning. No text.

Just a knock.

Vaani opened the door, pretending to be annoyed. "You again? People are going to think you live here."

He leaned lazily against the doorframe, a smirk dancing at the edge of his lips. His guitar case hung loosely from one shoulder.

"Let them. Maybe someone writes poetry about it."

She crossed her arms. "You do realize this is dangerously close to becoming a rom-com."

Aakash grinned. "Good. It's about time for the montage scene, don't you think?"

She rolled her eyes but stepped aside. "Fine. But you better not sing something from *Kuch Kuch Hota Hai.*"

"No promises," he called as he walked in.

The golden spill of early evening light wrapped itself around the furniture, touching the bookshelf spines and the chipped coffee table with soft reverence. The scent of jasmine floated from the candle Vaani lit on instinct, half to soothe herself, half to disguise the sudden electricity clinging to the air.

She sat cross-legged on the sofa, the cardigan she wore earlier abandoned, revealing a simple cotton tee. Her fingers fidgeted with the tassel of a cushion. Her breath? Slightly uneven.

Aakash settled across from her, the guitar resting on his thigh. He tuned it slowly, his gaze half on her, half on the strings. The movements were deliberate, practiced. His hands moved like they had done this a thousand times, but still treated the instrument like something holy.

"Ready?" he asked, not looking up.

She nodded. "I've been."

He started playing.

The first notes were unsure. Then steady. Then alive.

His voice followed—not pitch-perfect, not theatrical—but warm. Deep. Like velvet softened by years. The melody was raw. The lyrics, sharper than she expected. A story unfolded through his chords. A girl who carried storms in her sighs. A boy who tried to sing through silences. A connection that didn't ask for fireworks, only the courage to stay.

Vaani leaned forward slowly, as if drawn by the gravity of the sound itself. One hand drifted to her chest. Her eyes shimmered. Her breath caught.

When the last chord dissolved into the fading orange of the room, she didn't speak for a long moment.

"That was beautiful," she said finally, her voice a whisper.

Aakash looked up, his expression unreadable. "It's about you."

She blinked. "Me?"

He nodded. "Started writing it the night we met. Finished it last night."

The room stilled.

Vaani rose, walked over without hesitation, and knelt before him. Her fingers gently reached for his hand. His skin was warm. Familiar.

"You don't know what that means to me," she said, voice trembling slightly. "No one's ever…"

"Seen you like this?" he finished softly.

She nodded.

He reached up, brushing a curl away from her face. "I see you, Vaani. Even the parts you're still learning to name."

They stayed there for a while. Not speaking. Not needing to.

Outside, the city's evening pulse quickened. Horns. Distant laughter. The shuffle of slippers against the wet street. But inside, time had slowed. Or maybe it had just chosen them.

Later that night, the city softened into something almost tender.

The rain never came, but the clouds lingered like old friends who didn't know how to leave. A hush fell over Colaba—not the absence of sound, but the presence of quiet. The kind that blooms only after rush hour has sighed its last and the shops have pulled down their shutters halfway, as if saying, *not quite goodbye.*

They walked along the promenade, their pace unhurried, shoulders close enough to brush with every third step. Aakash carried the guitar case loosely over his back, like a satchel of secrets. Vaani carried nothing but the buzz in her chest.

The sea murmured beside them, rolling in and out with its ancient patience. The air smelled of salt, old rain, and something like clove oil from a distant street vendor. In the distance, a chaiwala poured steaming tea into steel glasses. The clink of glass on steel rang out like punctuation in the silence.

They bought one cup and shared it without discussion.

Vaani took the first sip, then handed it to him. He drank without hesitation. No ceremony. No nerves. Just a kind of shared stillness.

"You know what I love about this city?" she asked after a long moment.

Aakash looked at her, the side of his face illuminated by the amber streetlamp.

She didn't wait for a prompt. "It glows in places people forget to look."

He smiled. "Like fireflies."

She paused. "Exactly like fireflies."

They turned down a narrow path that branched away from the main promenade—less lit, more overgrown. The sound of the sea dimmed. Here, behind a low wall fringed with wild bougainvillea and peepal leaves, the world felt secret.

Golden flecks shimmered in the bushes.

Tiny glimmers. Blinking. Fading. Returning.

Fireflies.

Vaani's eyes widened. She let out a breath that sounded like wonder. "They don't need attention," she whispered. "They just… glow."

Aakash watched her more than the fireflies.

"Like you," he said, voice low, sincere.

She turned to him sharply. "You keep saying things that make it hard to breathe."

"Maybe breathing's overrated."

She smiled. Her heart thudded with too many things to name. "Tell me something real."

He looked away briefly, as if gathering courage from the sea. "I haven't felt safe like this in years. Haven't let someone this close to the raw parts."

She didn't interrupt.

"What changed?" she asked softly.

"You," he said. No embellishment. Just truth.

Her hand found his without thinking. Fingers laced easily. Gently.

"Then let's stay soft," she said.

They returned to her place just past midnight, their steps quieter now, like they were moving through something sacred. The streets had emptied, the shops shut, leaving behind only flickering neon signs and the scent of wet concrete. The electricity between them wasn't loud—it buzzed beneath the skin, in glances that lingered, in hands that brushed but didn't hold. Yet.

Vaani unlocked the door, letting them into her flat without ceremony. She didn't turn on the overhead light—only the corner lamp with the beige shade that cast the room in soft gold.

On the balcony, she stood facing the city.

Aakash stood behind her, just far enough not to touch, just close enough to feel.

The silence stretched—tentative, pulsing.

Then, as if pulled by a current too quiet to fight, his hands brushed her waist.

She turned slowly.

Their faces were inches apart.

"I should go," he whispered, the words not matching the way his eyes begged to stay.

"You don't want to," she said.

"No."

"Then don't."

And then she kissed him.

Or maybe he kissed her.

It didn't matter.

Their mouths found each other with a kind of urgency that wasn't rushed—it was hungry, but careful. A deepening, not a race. Her fingers slid into his curls. His hands found the small of her back. The world collapsed quietly around them.

Inside, they stumbled to the couch, laughter and breath mixing, kisses landing between soft gasps and murmured words neither would remember later. Her shirt was the first to go. Then his. Their hands fumbled—not clumsily, but like two people unlocking a code they hadn't been taught but somehow understood.

On the couch, they fell into each other. Their skin spoke what words couldn't. There was reverence in the way he touched her, as if he'd waited his whole life to get it right. Her fingers traced his shoulders, his jaw, like committing a poem to memory.

"Vaani," he whispered, his voice almost breaking.

"You undo me," she whispered back, pulling him closer. "Then stay undone."

When they moved together, it wasn't fireworks. It wasn't chaos. It was a slow, burning thing—like writing a verse on old parchment with trembling fingers. Every breath, every shift, every kiss felt like a word carefully chosen. They weren't in a rush. They weren't performing. They were just... learning each other. Like language. Like prayer.

Later, when the room had stilled and their limbs were tangled, breath shallow and hearts too full for speech, she pressed her lips to his shoulder and asked softly, "Do you believe in soulmates?"

Aakash turned his head, eyes dark and open. "I believe in *this*. Whatever it is."

She smiled, eyes closed. "Then let's believe together."

And beneath the flicker of a single bedside lamp, with the city stretching around them and the scent of jasmine still hanging in the air, the night became a promise.

Chapter Four

Rain Between the Lines

Mumbai's skies broke open without warning on Wednesday afternoon, as if the clouds had finally tired of holding it in. The rain came in heavy, diagonal sheets—wild, unapologetic. The kind that made shopkeepers rush to pull down shutters and schoolchildren scream with glee as they ran barefoot through puddles. The kind of rain that blurred windshields, soaked love letters, and softened every sharp edge the city had tried to wear like armor.

From her window seat, Vaani watched it fall.

Her apartment smelled faintly of petrichor and cardamom. The rain drummed steadily against the glass, louder than her thoughts but not loud enough to drown them. The sky outside had turned to ink, painted in thick strokes. She was curled beneath a cotton throw, her legs folded beneath her, an oversized maroon sweatshirt hanging loose on her frame. Damp hair clung to the back of her neck, curling rebelliously with the humidity. A hot mug of masala chai steamed softly on the windowsill beside her—half-sipped, already forgotten.

She had opened her notebook nearly twenty minutes ago. It still sat on her lap, blank. A pen tapped against the edge of the page, not writing but keeping rhythm with her restlessness.

She wasn't thinking about her assignment.

She was thinking about a kiss.

About fingers brushing ink-stained skin. About a boy with tired eyes and a guitar case full of unsaid things. A boy who hadn't messaged her today.

Aakash.

They hadn't labeled what this was. They hadn't needed to. The closeness had built itself, slowly but insistently—like ivy finding cracks in an old wall. One glance at a time. One chai cup passed hand to hand. One kiss by the sea. It had felt inevitable.

But now, there was silence.

Not dramatic silence. Not fight-born, angry silence. Just… space. Unexplained. The kind that lets doubt sneak in.

She reached for her phone again.

Still nothing.

Her thumb hovered over the messaging screen for a moment, tempted to send something casual. *Hey, the rain misses you too.* But she didn't. She didn't want to come off needy. Didn't want to disturb whatever rhythm he was in. Still, the silence was beginning to feel like rejection in slow motion.

She sighed, tugging the collar of her sweatshirt higher around her neck.

Across the narrow street, behind rain-misted glass, Aakash sat cross-legged on his bed, the pale grey light falling softly over the curve of his jaw. His guitar rested on his lap, strings untouched. He'd been meaning to play—really play—for the last hour. But every time his fingers found the chords, the melody collapsed before it could rise.

The window beside him was wide open, letting the rain's music pour in unfiltered. The scent of wet stone filled the room. His curtains fluttered like restless thoughts.

A sealed envelope sat on his nightstand. Not new. Worn at the corners. Faintly creased, like it had been opened and closed too many times.

The sender's name: *Ishita*.

A name from a time when he still believed love was linear. When the songs he wrote had clean endings.

He stared at the envelope for a long moment. The paper seemed to hum with memory. Not pain exactly—just the quiet discomfort of unfinished things. Of echoes that hadn't quite faded.

He reached over and slid the drawer shut with a soft but deliberate scrape.

Then he picked up his phone.

Typed: *Hey, want to come over? Rain's good company.*

Paused.

Deleted.

Typed again: *You busy? Got music and Maggi.*

Deleted.

He sighed.

Finally, he typed the simplest thing he could think of.

You free?

And hit send before he could convince himself not to.

Vaani's phone buzzed.

Just once.

You free?

Two words.

But they loosened something clenched in her chest. She reread them three times, unsure why they meant so much when they said so little. It wasn't poetry. It wasn't a declaration. But in that moment, it was everything.

Her fingers moved before her thoughts could catch up.

On my way, she typed.

She tossed the throw aside, barely registering the chill in the air. Her kurta was light, not rain-proof, and her sandals were already damp from the last time she'd stepped onto the balcony. But she didn't care. She grabbed her phone, stuffed it into her cloth sling bag, and bolted down the staircase, skipping the last two steps like she always did.

By the time she crossed the narrow street, her clothes were soaked. The rain greeted her like a playful enemy—persistent, wild, and completely indifferent to her attempt at staying dry. Her hair clung to her face. Her dupatta flapped behind her like a defiant flag. Her sandals squelched with every hurried step.

Aakash opened the door before she could knock.

She stood there, dripping, laughing breathlessly, cheeks flushed, eyes alight. She looked like a storm wrapped in skin.

He froze.

"You're drenched," he said, blinking as if she had stepped out of a dream.

"You're observant," she retorted, pushing past him with a grin and a dramatic shiver.

He shut the door, still stunned.

From the back of a chair, he tossed her a faded blue towel. "You'll catch a cold."

"I'll catch memories," she said, patting her arms dry. "You inviting me over in the middle of a monsoon? Bold move."

"I made chai," he replied, holding up a cup like a peace offering.

She sniffed the air dramatically. "Bribery by tea. The oldest trick in the book."

"Premium cutting chai," he said with mock gravity. "Sip slowly. It's a sacred art."

He handed her a steaming steel cup. Their fingers brushed again. And even through the damp towel and the fogged windows and the sharp scent of ginger, that one touch stole the breath right out of her.

She took a careful sip. "Extra ginger," she said, pleasantly surprised.

He nodded. "Had a feeling you'd need it."

They moved toward the small seating area. The floor was scattered with guitar picks and books and one sock she wisely chose not to comment on. The window behind them streaked with rainwater. Outside, the sky thundered distantly.

Inside, something quieter was stirring.

Their laughter filled the space—soft, slow, deliberate. It wasn't just noise. It was warmth. It was return.

Vaani curled up in one corner of the couch, knees pulled close. Aakash leaned against the window frame, his guitar beside him.

The rain didn't let up.

But for the first time all day, she didn't mind.

Aakash leaned against the window frame, his guitar within easy reach. Rain traced long, glistening lines down the glass beside him, catching reflections of streetlights and the flicker of passing headlights below. The city was a moving painting beyond the pane—gray and gold and wet and alive.

"I want you to hear something," he said suddenly, his voice lower than before. Not shy. Just careful.

Vaani straightened on the couch, her chai resting on the floor beside her. "I'm listening."

He picked up the guitar.

No lyrics. No introduction.

Just chords.

At first, simple—then gradually layered, uncertain, and beautiful in their brokenness. The melody wandered, like it wasn't sure where it was going but didn't want to stop. There were pauses that weren't mistakes. Silences that said more than notes.

It felt like memory and mourning and hope braided into one.

By the time he let the last note fade into the hush of the room, Vaani was sitting forward, her hands clasped between her knees, her expression unreadable.

She let the silence linger a moment longer before she spoke.

"That sounded... like missing," she said softly.

He exhaled. Slowly. Like something had loosened inside him. "It is."

She didn't rush him. Just waited.

It took a few more beats before he looked up, fingers still resting on the strings.

"There was someone," he said.

She nodded gently, letting the words arrive on their own.

"Ishita," he added, like the name had to be spoken to stop haunting him. "We were... serious. At least I thought we were. She wanted certainty. Timelines. A life planned in bullet points."

"And you?"

"I was still figuring out my chords."

He looked down at his hands. At the strings. At anything but her.

"She didn't leave all at once. That would've been easier. She left in pieces. Became quieter. Started editing who she was around me. Until one day, all that was left was a version of her I didn't recognize—and a version of me I didn't want to be."

Vaani listened, unmoving.

"She's not the villain," he added quickly. "She just needed someone who had answers. And I still had... songs."

He let the words trail off. The rain filled the silence like breath.

"She stayed long enough to become a ghost in every song," he murmured.

Vaani set her tea down and crossed the room slowly. She sat beside him but didn't crowd him. Her hand reached out, just brushing his knuckles.

"You're allowed to have ghosts," she said, her voice a feather in the storm.

He looked at her then.

Truly looked.

"You feel like a second chance," he said, his voice catching. "But I'm terrified I'll mess it up."

She turned her palm, letting his hand rest fully in hers. "Then don't."

Simple. But it held weight.

Like a spell.

Like a promise.

He didn't speak for a while after that.

Neither did she.

They sat there, side by side, fingers interlaced, the world slipping away behind the curtain of rain. No music now. No laughter. Just presence. Just two people who had told the truth and were brave enough to stay after it.

Then slowly, almost cautiously, he turned to her. Their faces were close—close enough for her to see the flicker of hesitation behind his eyes, the edge of an apology that hadn't been spoken yet.

"Vaani," he said, barely more than a breath. "Tell me to stop if…"

"Don't stop," she whispered, already closing the distance. "Not unless you want to."

"I don't."

And then he kissed her.

It was slow at first—like they were still getting used to the idea of each other in motion. But when she slid her hands into his hair and tilted her face closer, it became unstoppable. Heavier. Braver.

His arms wrapped around her waist, drawing her closer until her body fit against his like lyrics finally finding their rhythm. Their breaths tangled. Their knees bumped. Her fingers curled into the back of his shirt.

They stumbled together, soft laughter slipping between kisses, until they found the bed.

It wasn't rushed.

It wasn't rehearsed.

It was exploration—two people drawing a map with their mouths, with their hands, with the hush between words.

His shirt came off first. Then hers.

Their skin warmed against each other, heat replacing the damp chill that had crept in with the rain.

She kissed the hollow of his throat.

He traced the arch of her back with reverent hands.

They didn't speak.

They didn't need to.

They had accepted and acknowledged each other—no explanations, no questions.

It was all there—in the gasp that escaped her lips, in the way his grip tightened when her mouth found his collarbone. In how they moved together, unsure yet perfect, like improvising music on an old piano neither had played before but both instinctively knew.

And when they finally stilled, wrapped in a blanket that smelled faintly of soap and dreams, Vaani lay with her head on his chest, listening to the rain and the steady, calming drumbeat of his heart.

"Do you regret coming over?" he asked, his voice low, threaded with something unspoken.

She shook her head, lips brushing his skin. "No. Do you?"

"Never."

She tilted her face up and looked at him, her fingertips tracing the line of his jaw, down to the scar on his neck he'd never told her about.

"Then let's not overthink it," she said.

He smiled, kissed her forehead.

"Deal."

Outside, the rain began to lighten—no longer a storm, just a murmur. The city sighed beneath it, softer now, cleaner. As if it too had shed a weight it had carried too long.

Inside, they stayed tangled in silence.

Not afraid of it anymore.

And in that hush—the breath between chapters—a new kind of beginning unfolded. One made not of grand declarations, but the smallest, most sacred thing of all:

The decision to stay.

Cracks in the Calm

The days that followed stitched themselves into a delicate kind of rhythm.

Aakash and Vaani found a strange, tentative peace in the mundane — morning glances exchanged over railings, late-night texts filled with lazy jokes and half-formed dreams, the soft spill of stray guitar chords bleeding into her study sessions. Theirs was a new tenderness, stitched carefully between shared silences and unspoken promises.

Burnt toast breakfasts. Accidental toe-touches beneath the Irani café table. Quick smiles passed like secret notes. It felt fragile, sacred, like a garden growing wildly between two cracked sidewalks.

It wasn't perfect.

It was real.

But peace, like monsoon rain in Mumbai, never lingered too long.

It started on a Sunday morning.

Vaani curled herself into the fraying window seat of her tiny apartment, balancing a chipped mug of lukewarm coffee on the windowsill. Her legs tucked beneath her, notebook sprawled across her lap, pen tapping absentmindedly against the margin.

The morning smelled of wet earth and impending heat. Downstairs, vendors shouted over the clatter of rickshaws. Across the lane, laundry hung limp and defeated on sagging lines.

She scrolled through Instagram without thinking. Mindless. Half-distracted.

Until a photo froze her thumb.

A candid. Three years ago.

Aakash.

Grinning. Wind in his hair.

His arms wrapped tightly around a girl with wild, laughing eyes. A girl whose smile spoke of ownership, of history.

The caption beneath it:

Forever sounds like him.

Vaani's heart stuttered. Just a tiny misstep. A crack in the calm she'd been cradling so carefully.

The username: **@ishitasinghofficial**

Blue tick verified.

Singer. Influencer. Delhi-based. Beautiful in the way that made you feel like you needed to apologize just for existing.

And her latest post, dated barely two days ago:

"Mumbai. For closure."

Vaani swallowed hard. Her coffee sat abandoned. Her phone suddenly felt heavier in her hand.

A knock broke her trance.

Mitali, her flatmate, leaned in, two steaming mugs of chai in hand. "Earth to drama queen. You've been glaring at your phone like it owes you rent."

Vaani blinked, setting her phone aside too quickly. "It's nothing."

Mitali smirked. "Nothing? That "nothing" looks like heartbreak with a WiFi connection."

Vaani exhaled, hugging the mug to her chest. "It's Aakash. Or... his past."

Mitali settled beside her. "Tell me."

Vaani hesitated, then showed her the post.

Mitali whistled low. "Yikes."

"She's here," Vaani said softly. "In Mumbai. For closure."

"And you're worried he's the closure."

Vaani shook her head, but the movement was too slow, too unsure.

Across the street, Aakash sat on the edge of his bed, staring blankly at the same post. The half-written song on his notebook blurred into meaningless loops of ink.

The envelope bearing Ishita's name still sat buried in his drawer, heavier today than it had ever been.

His fingers hovered over his phone.

Typed: *Hey, can we talk?*

Deleted.

Typed again: *Miss you already. Don't freak out.*

Deleted.

Finally, he chose the only truth he had:

You free?

And sent it.

The rain came first — a low, grey mist rolling over the rooftops.

Vaani saw her phone light up.

You free?

Not poetry. Not a grand apology. Just two words.

But somehow, it steadied the storm that had risen inside her.

On my way, she typed back before doubt could sink its claws in.

She crossed the lane under a borrowed umbrella, sandals splashing through puddles. Aakash opened the door before she knocked—just like last time.

He looked tired.

He looked beautiful.

She stepped inside.

They didn't talk right away.

He brewed chai. She watched the rain bead down the windows. The silence between them was full, not empty. Brimming with everything they didn't know how to ask yet.

When the tea was ready, he passed her a cup.

She took it, hands brushing.

They sat on opposite ends of the couch.

He spoke first.

"I saw the post too."

Vaani nodded. "I figured."

"I didn't know she was coming."

"It's okay," she said, voice even. "You're allowed a past."

He looked at her like he was about to say something sacred.

"I don't want her."

She smiled tightly. "Maybe not. But memories have long shadows."

Aakash set his cup down carefully.

"I don't want to lose you because of old ghosts."

Vaani's eyes shimmered, but she blinked it away. "Some ghosts stay whether we want them to or not."

A long pause settled between their silences, thick as rain.

Rain pressed against the windows.

"Do you want to see her?" Vaani asked finally.

Aakash hesitated. Pain flickered across his face.

"I don't know."

Honest.

It hurt more because it was honest.

Vaani stood.

"Then figure it out," she said, gently. "I'll be here. Or I won't. But you need to know first."

She kissed his forehead — soft, aching.

And left.

That night, Mumbai's skyline blurred with mist.

Across the street, Vaani sat curled into her window seat, journal in her lap.

She wrote one line:

Sometimes, the bravest thing you can do is love someone enough to let them choose.

No tears.

Just a sigh.

Across the street, Aakash reached for the envelope in his drawer.

And opened it.

The past bled out in blue ink and broken promises.

He read it once. Twice. Then folded it carefully.

And let it fall into the rain.

It landed with a soft splash against the street — swept away, finally, by a city that never held onto anything for too long.

In the soft hush that followed, he picked up his guitar.

And wrote his first song that didn't have her name hidden inside it.

Distance in the Silence

The week that followed stretched like an unanswered question—long, quiet, heavy with things unsaid. Where once there had been rhythm—texts like breath, casual glances filled with meaning, laughter bubbling up without invitation—there was now static. Words came slower, glances slipped like water, and silences no longer felt like comfort. They felt like consequence.

It wasn't that Vaani and Aakash had fought. There were no harsh words, no raised voices, no grand gestures of anger. Just a slow unraveling. A drifting. A distance stitched together by small moments of hesitation. Missed replies. Ghosted goodnights. Inside jokes that no longer landed. Questions left on read.

They hadn't stopped caring. But caring had become quiet.

Vaani threw herself into college as if it were the only sturdy thing left. Her days became a blur of packed lecture halls and half-hearted group projects. She volunteered for everything—debates, library sorting, even a heritage walk she forgot to show up for. Her calendar looked impressive. Her energy, not so much.

She wasn't sleeping well. Her journals—once bursting with scribbles and late-night stanzas—now sat closed on her desk like artifact from a past life. She couldn't bring herself to write anything down. Every time she picked up a pen, it felt like admitting something was broken. And if she wrote about it, it would become real.

She didn't want real.

So she distracted herself.

She sat in the front row again. Her professors noticed her new punctuality, her precise notes, the way she no longer lingered after class with her headphones on and a silly grin across her face.

"Focused," one of them said. "Finally channeling your full potential."

If only they knew. She wasn't focused. She was hiding.

And hiding, Vaani discovered, was exhausting.

Even her friends didn't quite know how to read her anymore. She'd show up for lunch breaks, nod at the right times, laugh when everyone else did. But she was barely there. Like a ghost trying to remember how to wear a body again.

One evening, her phone lit up.

Aakash.

Just the name on the screen made her breath catch in her throat.

She didn't answer.

She stared at the screen, heart thudding like it was made of glass. Her thumb hovered over the green icon for a second too long. She told herself she needed more time. Just one more day. Just one more hour. Just until she didn't feel like falling apart at the sound of his voice.

The call went silent.

A moment later, a message.

I miss you.

Three words.

Simple. Bare. Honest.

She clutched the phone in both hands, as if it might slip through her fingers and vanish into the floor. Her eyes burned, but no tears came. Only the ache. That deep, dull ache that lives somewhere between the ribs. Where words get stuck. Where memory gnaws quietly.

She didn't reply.

Instead, she powered off the phone.

Slid it under her pillow.

Buried it like a secret too sacred—and too sore—to touch.

Thursday arrived wearing grey like mourning.

Mumbai, usually loud with urgency, moved sluggishly under a sky heavy with unshed rain. The breeze felt damp, carrying the scent of wet earth and old dust. Even the crows seemed quieter, their usual complaints swallowed by the thick clouds pressing low over the buildings.

Vaani walked the college gardens with Meera, dragging her fingertips across damp hibiscus petals as they passed. The air was cool, the ground squelching slightly beneath their sandals, and the gulmohar trees bowed low as if exhausted by the weight of the season.

Meera had been patient—too patient. She'd watched Vaani drift through classes like a girl underwater. She hadn't asked until now, but she could no longer ignore the way her best friend's eyes had dulled. The way her words now came pre-shrunk, measured, careful.

"You haven't smiled in days," Meera said finally, her voice low, gentle, almost apologetic for pointing it out.

Vaani offered a weak curve of her lips, more gesture than expression. "I'm smiling now."

"No, you're performing," Meera said, stopping beneath a drooping tree. "That's your don't-ask-me smile. Your 'I'm fine, now shut up' smile. It's not real."

They sat on a weathered stone bench under the tree's sweeping branches, the world around them muted. Leaves rustled half-heartedly. The puddles nearby reflected fractured images of buildings and sky.

"I feel like I'm stuck in someone else's story," Vaani said suddenly. "Like... like I'm not the main character anymore. Like I'm just watching from a distance while everything crumbles."

Meera didn't answer right away. She just reached over and slipped her hand into Vaani's. Her grip was warm, grounding.

"That's heartbreak, love," she said after a beat. "It's not always fire and screaming. Sometimes it's just silence. Sometimes it's forgetting how to be the heroine for a while."

Vaani tilted her face toward the sky, eyes blinking rapidly against the thick clouds.

"I thought I knew him," she whispered.

"You did," Meera replied. "You knew the version of him he gave you. We all do that, Vaani. We fall for the part of someone they're willing to show us. Doesn't make it any less real."

Vaani's voice cracked on the next question. "Then why let me get that close? Why let me build dreams over quicksand?"

Meera's fingers tightened around hers.

"Because sometimes," she said softly, "we don't realize we're still bleeding until someone tries to hold us."

Vaani looked down at their clasped hands. She didn't cry. Not yet. But her shoulders slumped, like something inside her had finally acknowledged it was tired of pretending not to be hurt.

Around them, the city moved on. Horns blared faintly in the distance. A student jogged past, holding an umbrella upside down in the rain just for laughs. Life didn't pause for heartbreak. But in that moment, beneath the gulmohar tree, two friends made space for it to breathe.

Across the narrow street, Aakash was unraveling— slowly, invisibly.

His flat, once noisy with guitar strums and the occasional off-key humming of old Bollywood classics, now echoed with absence. The walls, bare of art but covered in scuff marks and nail holes, stared back at him with quiet judgment. Even the ceiling fan seemed to spin more listlessly than usual.

He sat on his bed for hours, knees drawn up, elbows resting on them, staring at nothing in particular. His guitar sat untouched in the corner, a thin layer of dust beginning to settle across its once-glossy neck. A half-filled cup of black coffee grew cold on the side table. The old vinyl player he loved had given up waiting—its silence now louder than any melody it could have offered.

He'd tried writing.

More than once.

He scribbled on napkins. Scraps of receipt paper. An old envelope that once held a greeting card from his mother. The words that came were fractured. Impatient. Either too raw or too hollow. A verse would begin and fall apart halfway through. Choruses became apologies he didn't know how to end.

Nothing fit.

Nothing stayed.

He missed her.

Not in the casual, flirty, *"I miss your chai habits"* kind of way. Not even in the aching, *"I wish you were next to me tonight"* kind of way.

He missed her in the breath between chords. In the echo of an empty mug on the kitchen counter. In the way his room no longer smelled like jasmine and old pages. In the hum of the city that felt louder now, as if trying to drown out the silence she'd left behind.

He missed the way she'd trace book spines without realizing it. The way she'd burn her tongue on hot chai and still insist it wasn't hot enough. How she'd go quiet right before saying something that mattered.

Vaani wasn't a memory.

She was a haunting.

And she was everywhere.

He got up suddenly, unable to sit still. Grabbed his hoodie. Didn't bother locking the flat door properly. The streets were damp from earlier rain, but the skies were dry now—just a low haze of smoke and old clouds.

He didn't think about where he was going.

His feet knew before he did.

Ten minutes later, he stood outside her gate.

There was no plan. No words. No grand gesture.

Just longing.

The soft golden glow from her bedroom spilled into the street like a trail he wasn't sure he was allowed to follow. Behind the curtains, a silhouette moved. Paused. Then vanished again.

He stayed there. Watching. Waiting. Breathing unevenly.

He didn't knock.

Didn't call.

Didn't send another text.

He just stood there—soaked in guilt, heavy with maybe's and if-only's.

Just a boy hoping for a girl who might not be his anymore.

And then, after ten long minutes that felt like a thousand, he turned.

And walked away.

The night swallowed him without ceremony.

That night, Vaani sat wrapped in a soft, faded shawl on her tiny porch swing, her bare feet tucked beneath her. The swing creaked gently with each movement, a familiar lullaby she didn't realize she needed. Above, the sky hung low and smog-soft, muffling the moon into a pale blur behind the clouds.

Even the city had gone quiet.

The dogs—usually loud, always restless—had curled up somewhere out of sight. The chaiwala from two lanes down had long shut his stall. Even the faint throb of traffic from the main road had dulled to a low, humming sigh. It was the kind of Mumbai night that made you feel like the only living soul in the city.

And Vaani felt every inch of that loneliness.

She sat with her arms wrapped around her knees, the shawl pooling like waves around her ankles. Her phone remained off, buried under layers of clothes in her closet now. She didn't want it glowing at her anymore, didn't want to flinch every time it buzzed. There was nothing left to wait for.

Above her, a single wind chime tapped out a half-rhythm in the damp air.

She wasn't crying. Not really.

Tears had come days ago—in the shower, in class, even mid-bite during lunch. But tonight, the grief had taken another shape. Heavier. Still. Like water that had flooded every crevice and now simply settled.

She thought of the first night.

The spilled chai. That crooked, cocky smile. The way he'd said her name like it already belonged in a song.

She thought of the swing set on the promenade. Of fireflies blinking like forgotten magic. Of the first kiss that felt like falling, and how she'd believed—just for a moment—that she'd finally landed in the right arms.

And now...

Now, she whispered the truth out loud, just once, just to the night.

"I wish he hadn't made it feel like forever... if he was only going to treat it like a pause."

Her voice didn't tremble. It was too tired for that.

The sadness no longer burned—it simply sat. Like a house no longer haunted, just abandoned.

She didn't hate him.

That was the hardest part.

She couldn't hate the boy who touched her like she was poetry. Who called her brave when she was just trying to stay afloat. Who told her she was a second chance, even if he didn't know what to do with one.

No, she didn't hate him.

She didn't even blame him.

Some loves don't die with screaming or betrayal.

Some just fade—soft, tired, and silent.

Across the street, Aakash sat by his window, legs drawn up on his bed, his hoodie damp from the walk he hadn't meant to take. He stared at the same stars, the same muted sky. Wondered if she was awake. Wondered if she missed him. Wondered if it was too late to try.

He reached for his guitar.

Strummed two notes.

Both wrong.

He placed it back down.

Even music couldn't find its way through the fog inside him.

And so he stayed there—quiet, unmoving.

She stayed on her swing, hands curled in her shawl.

And the space between them remained vast, invisible, and unbearable.

Because sometimes love ends not with a goodbye…

…but with two people sitting beneath the same sky,

wishing the silence didn't feel so much like loss.

Her Own Shadow

Sleep had become a stranger Vaani no longer knew how to invite in.

Night after night, she lay awake long past the hour when the city gave up its noise. Past the barking of stray dogs, the final mop swipes from the building watchman, the last train's distant wail. She would lie still—motionless on the outside but brimming with thought inside, like a kettle left on low flame, just shy of boiling over.

Her thoughts betrayed her most when the lights were off. That was when memory crept in—not violent, just persistent. A soft thief, replaying moments with cruel precision. His hand brushing hers near the chai stall. The way he said her name that first night. The warmth in their silences, now gone sharp with absence.

Vaani stared at the ceiling as the fan overhead, shadows casting slow circles across the wall. She felt like she was spinning too—stuck between what was and what might never be. The ache wasn't loud anymore. It had found a rhythm in her bones, like muscle memory. Familiar. Inevitable. She traced one fingertip along the bedsheet, as if a new story might rise from the thread.

She gave up on sleep around 3:00 AM.

The desk lamp clicked on with a low buzz, casting her room in a muted glow. She sat at her study table, her legs folded beneath her, a blanket draped across her shoulders. The glow from her laptop pulsed gently—one line blinking at the top of a half-written paper she hadn't touched in three days. It blinked like a heartbeat, steady and judgmental.

Her textbooks lay open around her in what might have passed for a hardworking scene—except none of the pages were being read. Her pen tapped a metronome rhythm against the edge of her notebook, the page inside untouched except for one scribbled line.

What if I'm just another chapter in his story?

The ink had smudged. She didn't remember when. Her hand had dragged across it earlier, maybe while she'd been rubbing her eyes. It looked like a bruise now—spilled across an otherwise clean page.

She sighed and closed the journal softly, as if it had somehow accused her. Even her own words felt traitorous now, heavy with doubt. She used to find comfort in writing, in pouring things out. But these days, everything she wrote felt like it might come back to hurt her.

In the quiet, her walls seemed closer. Even the breeze that came in from the slightly ajar window felt hesitant, like it didn't know how to offer comfort anymore.

College had become her hiding place. A stage for rehearsed normalcy. She arrived early. Sat at the front. Took notes like her scholarship depended on it. Nodded when professors looked for eye contact. Showed up at every group meeting and left before anyone could notice how quiet she'd become.

To her classmates, she was a picture of renewed focus.

To herself, she was an echo.

In the hallways, she floated—greeting people with half-smiles, dodging conversations she once loved. In the canteen, she sat at her usual spot but barely touched her food, picking at it while laughter and gossip buzzed around her like a world she could no longer access.

And every evening, as the sun dipped into the sea and painted Colaba in soft orange, she'd sit by her window, heart in hand, waiting.

Not expecting, but still waiting.

For a knock. A call. A message. A sign.

Anything that might remind her that she hadn't just imagined it all.

But the ache stayed. Like a familiar guest overstaying its welcome. No dramatic fights. No closure. Just distance— a silence that kept feeding itself.

She had become a girl in limbo. Half in the past, half pretending to be fine in the present. And every day, she slipped a little more into the version of herself that smiled at strangers and broke down in restrooms.

She was becoming her own shadow.

It was a Wednesday when Meera finally cracked.

The two of them sat in their usual corner of the college canteen, tucked beneath a ceiling fan that never spun fast enough and beside a window that overlooked the crowded street. Outside, an auto honked, someone dropped a steel plate, and a student group argued over whether ketchup belonged on dosa.

Inside, the air between them felt tighter than usual.

"You look like you haven't eaten anything but iced coffee and overthinking," Meera said, sliding onto the bench across from Vaani. She dropped a plate of steaming samosas between them with the authority of a woman declaring war on avoidance. The grease had already begun to seep through the paper plate, staining the tray beneath it.

Vaani attempted a smile. A polite, weary thing.

"I'm fine. Just tired."

Meera arched a brow, the kind that could cut glass. "Tired of what—sleep or your own head?"

Vaani didn't answer. Her hands toyed with a crumpled napkin, tearing it into smaller and smaller pieces, like trying to make the chaos more manageable. Her eyes flicked to the side as someone passed by with a guitar case slung over their shoulder.

That was all it took.

Meera sighed, not unkindly, and reached across the table to gently clasp her friend's hand.

"Talk to me."

The silence stretched. Then Vaani's voice arrived, quiet and trembling at the edges.

"Do you ever feel like you let someone in too soon? Before you figured yourself out?"

Meera's thumb moved over her knuckles, slow and grounding. "Every heartbreak starts there, Vaani. But that doesn't make the love wrong. Sometimes, it just means the timing was."

Vaani looked up, her eyes glassy but dry. "I don't even know if it was love. It was… lightning. Sudden. Bright. Beautiful. But it burned. And now it's only smoke I can't breathe around."

Meera leaned back, absorbing the words. "That sounds a lot like love to me."

Vaani blinked, unsure whether that comforted or hurt her more.

"I keep wondering if I imagined the good parts," she admitted. "Like maybe it was only magic because it was short-lived. Maybe if it had gone on longer, it would've cracked anyway."

"Or maybe," Meera said gently, "it was real in the moment. And that's what's making it hard to let go."

The noise of the canteen continued around them, a blur of clinking glasses, orders shouted in half-English, and phones buzzing on tables. But the space between them felt sacred, soft-edged.

Vaani let out a shaky breath. "It's like I'm still glowing from it… even though it hurts. Like I don't want to put it out, but I don't know how to live with it either."

Meera's voice dropped to a whisper. "Then don't put it out. Not yet. Just learn to live near the warmth without reaching for the flame."

There was something in the way she said it that loosened the knot in Vaani's chest. Like Meera had built a small, safe room in her sentence. A room where grief could sit down without being asked to leave.

They didn't speak after that.

Vaani took a small bite of the samosa. It wasn't hot anymore. But it was comforting.

And maybe, that was enough.

That night, Vaani didn't plan to go anywhere.

She told herself she'd stay in. Read a few pages of a novel she'd already abandoned. Scroll through her camera roll until sleep found her. Maybe light a candle, maybe not. But her body had other plans.

Sometimes grief moves through us without asking for permission.

She found herself walking. No destination. No playlist. Just the hush of the city's late-night rhythm and her breath—uneven, but steady.

Past shuttered shops, where mannequins in cracked glass windows stared blankly into the night. Past hawkers rolling up tarpaulin sheets, their voices hushed with fatigue. Past lovers leaning against parked bikes, sharing secrets too soft for the world.

And eventually, toward the sea.

The promenade opened up like a held breath.

Waves greeted her with their usual insistence, licking the edge of the stone wall with relentless devotion. The sky stretched wide, painted in bruised navy and stardust. The moon hid behind clouds, playing peek-a-boo with the tide. Streetlights buzzed softly, casting halos onto the wet path.

She walked slowly.

The city's pulse slowed here.

Mumbai, chaotic and sharp-edged by day, always felt different by the sea. Softer. More forgiving. Like it understood heartbreak better than most places.

She found the bench.

Their bench.

It looked different now. Smaller. Not in size, but in presence. Without him beside her, it had lost its gravity. She sat slowly, pulling her sweater sleeves over her fingers, hugging her knees close.

The stone was cold beneath her. But she didn't mind. The cold kept her honest.

For a while, she just listened. To the sea. To the distant horn of a ferry. To the wind whispering secrets across the water.

In her mind, she let him sit beside her. Just for a moment.

Not the version who stopped texting. Not the silence that filled her inbox like fog.

But the boy who looked at her like she was a song he hadn't figured out the lyrics to yet.

She could picture it so clearly—him beside her, humming under his breath, fingers tapping out chords on his knee, that half-sarcastic smile tugging at the edge of his mouth. The way he would've nudged her shoulder. Tucked her hair behind her ear. Said something dumb and poetic in the same breath.

But there was no shoulder nudge. No fingers in her hair. No crooked grin.

Just wind. Just waves. Just her.

And when the memory of him settled fully into her chest, she whispered it—honest, soft, painful:

"I don't hate you, Aakash… but I don't know if I trust you either. And I don't know what hurts more."

The words didn't echo.

They weren't meant to.

They just dissolved—carried away by the salt air, swept into the tide, like a message in a bottle that didn't need to be found.

She stayed there for a long time.

Long enough for joggers to pass. For a chai vendor to call out one last order before packing up. For the wind to shift direction, and with it, something inside her.

It wasn't closure.

It wasn't healing.

It was space.

Space between the memory and the ache.

A moment to exist without performing strength.

A bench, a sea, a girl, and the truth.

And for now—that was enough.

When Vaani finally stood, her legs felt stiff.

The sea breeze had curled itself around her, tugging gently at her sweater and tangling her hair into small, wet knots. Her palms were cold. Her back ached from sitting still for too long. But her chest—her chest felt lighter in a way she hadn't expected.

Not healed. Not yet. But something had loosened.

The grief was still there. The ache hadn't disappeared. But it had changed shape—grown less jagged, less urgent. What had once felt like drowning now felt like treading water. And that was something.

She began walking again, slow at first. One step, then another. Not away from anything. Just forward.

Past the swing set where they'd once kissed under the low, golden lamplight.

Past the railing where he'd traced her fingers with his.

Past the world they had built in pieces—now scattered like beach glass. Still beautiful, but no longer sharp.

She didn't replay the conversations. Didn't reach for the old texts. Didn't rehearse what she would say if he ever showed up again. Tonight, she didn't need answers. She didn't need explanations. She only needed her feet to keep moving. Her breath to keep coming. Her heart to remember how to beat for her, not for the absence of him.

Back in her room, the air smelled faintly of lavender. The lamp still glowed, its light soft and forgiving.

She peeled off her sweater, kicked off her sandals, and slipped into bed without turning her phone back on.

She didn't reach for her journal.

Didn't scroll through old photos.

She lay still.

And for the first time in a long time, she didn't feel the need to cry herself to sleep.

The pain was still there—curled into the edges of her like a sleeping cat—but it no longer scratched.

Maybe this was healing. Not grand. Not cinematic. Just surviving a little more each night. Letting the pain fade from scream to murmur. From flame to ember.

Maybe she wasn't ready to forget him yet.

But she was learning to remember herself.

And that?

That was a beginning.

Chapter Eight

The Arrival of Reyan

The morning after her night walk to the sea face, Vaani woke with an ache that wasn't quite physical. It didn't press into her bones or throb at her temples like a fever. It floated—just above her chest—like a weightless bruise. Present. Lingering. Unnamed.

Her dreams had been paper-thin–fractured visions of rain-slicked streets. A bench that whispered. A guitar string snapping. A boy turning away, again and again, always before she could speak.

She awoke with her pillow askew, her blanket half-kicked to the floor, and the distinct feeling that she'd been holding her breath for hours.

The room smelled like lavender and unresolved emotions.

She blinked against the grey light filtering through her curtains, feeling disoriented—not in body, but in meaning. Her thoughts came slow, like a lazy tide. Just when she was reaching for sleep again, her phone buzzed once. Then twice.

She flipped it over.

Professor Luthra: *Vaani, I've recommended you to assist an alumnus who's visiting for a short guest lecture series. He'll need help prepping for sessions. Brilliant writer—comes from Delhi. Name's Reyan Kaul. Please meet him at the department office at 11 a.m.*

She reread the message twice.

Part of her wanted to sigh. Another obligation. Another stranger. Another thing she had to show up for—when all she really longed for was to retreat into the quiet of last night, to dissolve into stillness, and let the sea erase her edges until she felt less like a person and more like a wave simply passing through.

But then she saw the name—*Luthra*—and that changed everything.

If there was one person whose words still reached her, it was him.

Professor Luthra had always seen through her defenses. Before she'd even admitted to herself that writing felt like breathing, he had called her a storyteller. Had circled her margin notes in red ink and written, *"Find the poem here, Vaani. It's hiding."* Had once quoted Neruda to her after she botched a presentation, saying, *"Let us forget with generosity, those who cannot love us."*

So, she replied.

Sure, sir.

It wasn't enthusiasm. But it was something.

By 10:45, Vaani stood in the English department corridor, notebook clutched like a lifeline. Her brown leather-bound journal had become a fixture—tucked under her arm, creased at the corners, its pages filled with raw scrawls no one else had read. It gave her the illusion of preparedness, even when her world felt uneven.

She wore a faded blue kurta, the kind that felt like home. Her silver jhumkas chimed with every small turn of her head, delicate music for her nerves. She hadn't put on eyeliner. Hadn't touched her lips with gloss. There was something honest about arriving as she was. She didn't feel the need to armor herself today.

The door to the department office creaked open.

She expected someone older. Grayer. Maybe formal, starched, with a clipboard and unnecessary authority.

She got Reyan Kaul.

Tall. Broad-shouldered. A silver watch peeking beneath the rolled-up sleeves of an olive-green shirt. Dark-rimmed glasses sat lightly on the bridge of his nose, accentuating the quiet intensity in his gaze. He didn't look like a guest lecturer. He looked like someone who read poetry at midnight but never admitted it. Someone who knew the difference between solitude and being forlorn— someone who had lived both.

He looked up from his phone.

And smiled.

"You must be Vaani."

His voice was warm—low, even—but not soft. There was a subtle confidence curled into each syllable, the kind that didn't need volume to hold attention. His Delhi accent touched the vowels with a lazy ease.

She blinked. "Yes. And you're... Reyan?"

"Guilty," he said, extending a hand.

She took it, surprised by the firm steadiness of his grip. Not overpowering. Just… sure.

"Professor Luthra said I'd be in good hands," he added. "Told me you're the best in the department."

She raised an eyebrow, lips twitching into a reluctant smile. "He says that to everyone. Don't fall for it."

"Too late," he said, grinning. "I'm already impressed."

There it was—that flicker. Quick. Barely there. But unmistakable. Not a spark. Not tension. Just recognition. That quiet sense of meeting someone whose presence doesn't jar you, but folds into the moment like it's always belonged.

She straightened, her voice easy but professional. "Well then, Reyan Kaul," she said, chin tilted slightly. "Let's get started."

In the days that followed, Reyan Kaul became a quiet rhythm in Vaani's routine.

He wasn't the kind of man who entered rooms with fanfare, but the spaces he inhabited always seemed to shift around him. His presence was a steady hum—low and constant—threading through lecture halls, library corners, and chai breaks with the kind of quiet assurance that drew attention without demanding it.

His sessions filled fast.

Not just because he was an alumnus or because the flyers said *published author* beneath his name. It was how he spoke. Measured. Thoughtful. As though each word was chosen with care, not for performance, but because it deserved to be heard.

He didn't just teach theory. He told stories. Sometimes about his time in Delhi—of bookstore basements and lonely rooftops and monsoon poetry readings. Other times about language itself. About how the right sentence can feel like touch. How silence between lines is sometimes the loudest part.

Students lingered after class to ask him questions they would never have dared to ask their full-time professors.

"Do you think writing ever stops hurting?" one girl asked once.

Reyan had smiled, just slightly. "It never stops hurting," he said. "But if you do it right, it starts healing too."

It wasn't just the students who noticed. Staff began referencing him during staffroom chatter.

"Sharp mind, that Kaul," someone said over ginger tea.

"Too sharp," another added. "Knows exactly when to stay quiet."

But it was how he listened that stayed with Vaani.

Not the polite, nod-along kind of listening she'd grown used to—people waiting for their turn to speak, or checking their phone while pretending to care. Reyan listened like her words had mass. Like they might shatter if he wasn't careful. She felt oddly exposed in his presence, but never unsafe.

They met every morning before his class. Sometimes for ten minutes, sometimes longer. He would jot down ideas on the back of used printouts, occasionally glance up to ask her if a particular phrasing sounded pretentious or honest.

"You always carry that notebook?" he asked one day, nodding toward the frayed brown leather journal she kept tucked under her arm like an armor.

She smiled. "I feel safer when it's with me."

"Do you ever let anyone read from it?"

She hesitated. "Rarely."

"Would you let me?"

There was no pressure in his voice. Just curiosity. Gentle and open.

She didn't answer right then.

But the next day, while they sat on the campus lawn under a blooming gulmohar, she tore a page from the back. Quietly. As if offering a secret.

A poem.

Short. Unrhymed. Raw.

About loss that lingered like steam. About silences that screamed. About the impossible guilt of starting to breathe again when someone else had stopped sharing the air.

Reyan read it in silence.

Once.

Then again.

Then he folded the page with care and placed it inside his notebook.

"You bleed, Vaani," he said softly. "Not everyone does. Most people echo what they think they're supposed to say. But you—you carve."

She didn't know what to say to that. No one had ever said something like that to her before.

Not her professors.

Not her peers.

Not even Aakash.

The words left her breathless—not in a swooning way, but in that deep, unsettling way that came from being deeply seen.

And still accepted.

It was pure coincidence.

Aakash had come to campus to meet his old friend Neel—borrow a worn-out textbook, maybe grab a cheap sandwich from the vendor near the gate. He hadn't planned on walking through the English department lawn. He certainly hadn't planned on seeing her.

But fate, ever the dramatist, had other ideas.

There she was.

Vaani.

Sitting on the edge of a stone bench, her back to the building, her journal resting loosely in her lap. Her hair was pulled back in a loose braid, strands escaping to curl near her temple. She wore a mustard-yellow kurta, sunlight catching in its creases like she'd been stitched into it. Her silver jhumkas danced faintly in the breeze.

And next to her—

Reyan.

Laughing. Talking. Leaning just close enough to suggest familiarity, but far enough to leave ambiguity room to stretch its claws.

They looked like a page from a novel someone had forgotten to tear out.

Not a dramatic scene. Nothing overly romantic.

But intimate in its comfort.

Aakash stood frozen behind a tree, half-shielded by its trunk, half-shielded by indecision. He wasn't proud of it—this voyeurism, this weakness—but he couldn't stop watching. Not yet.

She was smiling.

A small, real smile. Not the one she wore when people asked how she was doing, or the one she gave to strangers in elevators. This smile reached her eyes. It softened her posture.

And it wasn't for him.

Something inside Aakash twisted, sharp and sudden.

He felt like a radio suddenly tuned to a frequency he couldn't quite understand. Like watching someone finish a puzzle he didn't know was missing pieces. There was no public display. No lingering touch. But the connection was visible. Subtle. Certain.

He didn't move. Not at first.

Just stood there, a ghost watching the living.

Then slowly—deliberately—he turned and walked away.

The ache followed.

It sat just beneath his ribs, stubborn as a lyric you can't forget. The memory of her laugh echoing in his chest like it had been meant for him. Once. Long ago. Or maybe just last month.

Back in his room, he closed the windows. Turned off the music. Sat on his bed and stared at his guitar.

He didn't touch it.

He didn't want to.

He reached for his phone instead.

That evening, the city wore its usual costume—headlights streaking across wet streets, horns impatient, rain clouds pacing but undecided. Mumbai was always on the brink of either collapse or poetry.

Vaani sat at her desk, a cup of tea gone cold beside her, the same page in her journal open for nearly half an hour.

But her hand didn't move yet.

She was still thinking about Reyan.

Not in the way one thinks of romantic futures or tangled feelings. Not yet. It was quieter than that. Slower.

His words echoed.

You carve.

She didn't even know how to hold a compliment like that. It had landed in her chest with the kind of impact, most declarations only pretend to have. Not because it was flattering, but because it was true.

Aakash had never said anything like that.

He had loved her in his own way—improvised and chaotic—but he had never made her feel like her silence had value, like her thoughts deserved to be preserved instead of just shared. With Reyan, there was no performative need. No urgency. Just… permission.

Permission to exist fully.

And that had shifted something.

She looked down at her open journal. This time, her pen moved.

She didn't write about Reyan.

She wrote about silence.

About the way it sometimes hugs too tight. About how memories fade in stages—first the sound of someone's voice, then their scent, and then finally, the reason why you stayed so long. About love that lingers like a borrowed shirt—familiar, warm, but not yours anymore.

She wrote until her hand cramped.

Then she paused.

Her phone buzzed.

Aakash: *I saw you today. At college. You looked… happy.*

For a moment, everything stilled.

Her breath hitched—not because she hadn't expected it, but because she had. That was the problem. The old script was still too easy to remember.

But the girl she was now?

She wasn't reading from that script anymore.

Her fingers hovered over the keypad.

Then slowly, she typed:

I'm trying to be.

She stared at the words for a full minute before pressing send.

No emoji.

No punctuation.

Just truth.

There was no reply.

She didn't expect one.

And for the first time in weeks, that felt okay.

She closed her journal. Switched off the lamp. Let the sounds of the city drift in through the open window—the distant murmur of rickshaws, the rustle of wind through half-wet leaves, a boy humming an old Kishore Kumar tune somewhere down the street.

And in that dusky in-between space—where memory curled against maybe—Vaani let herself begin again.

Not with someone.

Not for anyone.

Just her.

And it was enough.

Chapter Nine

Fractures and Falsettos

Aakash didn't sleep that night.

Not in the way most people understood sleep. His body remained still beneath the tangled sheets, but his mind never stopped pacing. It spun and looped, like a carousel refusing to power down, each thought dragging the next, each memory colliding with the last.

Outside, the rain tapped out a sharp, restless rhythm against the windowpanes. It wasn't soft or romantic. It was unrelenting. A harsh percussion that echoed the noise inside him.

He turned to his side. Then to the other. He adjusted the pillow once, then twice. Nothing worked. Nothing softened the ache.

His phone, laid facedown beside him, blinked with the same quiet persistence.

He reached for it, thumb already unlocking it out of habit. The last message still glared at him like a wound.

Vaani: *I'm trying to be.*

It wasn't cruel. It wasn't distant.

But it wasn't soft either.

It was tired. It was honest. And it carried the kind of resignation that settled behind a locked door—just loud enough to be heard but too far to be answered.

He read it again.

And again.

As if a new meaning might bloom between the lines if he stared long enough. But all it gave him was the same sting—the same realization that she was slipping through his fingers, and he had no idea how to ask her to stay without breaking her more.

His fingers hovered. Typed. Deleted.

I'm sorry.

Deleted.

I miss you more than I know how to say.

Deleted.

Can we just start over?

Deleted.

It wasn't that he didn't feel it. He just didn't trust any of it to come out right.

The cursor blinked at him, steady and merciless.

Finally, with a frustrated sigh, he tossed the phone aside. It landed softly against the pillow beside him, casting a brief blue light before it went dark again.

3:11 a.m.

His fingers twitched, aching for his guitar, but he didn't move. He couldn't. The strings would sound like regret tonight, and he wasn't sure he could survive hearing that out loud.

Across the city, at nearly the same hour, Vaani sat alone in the back corner of the college library, surrounded by the scent of old books and the quiet rustle of pages turning in other lives.

Her laptop was open, an article on feminist literary theory blinking from the screen, but she wasn't reading. Not really. Her pen twirled absently between her fingers, its movement mindless. Her gaze stayed locked on the far window, where the light rain blurred the view into a watercolour painting of campus trees and slate-grey sky.

Her headphones rested lightly in her ears. A voice note played—a poem Reyan had sent that morning.

He had layered it over soft piano chords. Just a few gentle notes beneath the weight of his voice. His tone was steady, not theatrical. It wasn't about impressing. It was about laying something down—simple and true.

I wrote this after the storm last night, he had said. *Not the one outside. The one I carry sometimes.*

She listened.

Once. Then again.

The poem was about forgiveness—forgiving oneself. About how we carry our younger versions like ghosts in our skin. About how healing isn't linear, but a soft undoing.

He didn't ask what she thought of it. He never did. He simply shared, without expectation, like tossing pebbles into a lake just to see the ripples.

And that, she realized, was the difference.

With Reyan, there was no ache of anticipation. No second-guessing.

He didn't make her heart race. He steadied it.

But some part of her—stubborn and bruised—still remembered the boy who made her believe in thunder and fire. Who kissed her like poetry. Who made promises with unfinished songs.

That part hadn't disappeared. It had just grown quiet. Like a violin waiting to be tuned again.

Two days passed.

Two full sunrises and sunsets—neither of which Vaani remembered watching.

She went through the motions. Lectures. Notes. Small smiles. Even Reyan's steady presence beside her felt like something she had to breathe into slowly, like a rhythm she hadn't yet learned how to trust.

Then, on a quiet afternoon, just after she had stepped out of the seminar hall and into a corridor pulsing with post-class chatter, her phone buzzed again.

Aakash: *Can we talk? Please.*

No poetry. No excuses.

Just two words carrying the full weight of a storm still circling overhead.

Vaani didn't respond. Not immediately.

She tucked the phone into her bag and walked—past the bulletin board, past the chai stand, past the same tree she once stood beneath when Aakash had sung an unfinished melody just for her. The memory rose like mist, soft and unwelcome.

For hours, she did nothing.

Then, without texting back, without telling anyone, she found herself at the place she'd promised herself she wouldn't return to so soon.

His house.

The route unfolded easily beneath her feet. Her body remembered it even if her heart wasn't sure. The familiarity unnerved her—the cracks in the pavement, the old red hibiscus bush near his gate, the wind that carried the faint scent of rain and regret.

She hesitated for only a breath before knocking—soft, hesitant.

The door opened instantly.

Aakash stood there, his eyes heavy, jaw rough with days of unshaved stubble, his hoodie rumpled as if he hadn't left the house in days.

He looked like someone who hadn't just been waiting for her—but needed her to arrive in order to breathe.

"I didn't think you'd come," he said, his voice low, raw around the edges.

She met his gaze. "I didn't think I would either."

They stood like that for a while—two silhouettes backlit by memories, facing each other with everything unsaid folding the space between them.

Inside, the living room was unchanged. But that was the problem.

It was untouched.

No new songs scribbled on paper. No coffee cups half-full. No fresh energy. Just stillness. A stillness that used to be comforting, now felt sterile.

She sat at one end of the couch. He settled at the other.

An invisible canyon yawned between them.

"I saw you with Reyan," he said, finally.

His voice wasn't accusatory. But it wasn't steady either.

Vaani didn't flinch. "He's my colleague."

"You seemed... close."

She looked at him squarely. "He listens."

Aakash's jaw twitched. "I did too. I tried to."

She shook her head gently, her voice painfully calm. "You didn't try, Aakash. You assumed. You assumed I'd wait. That I'd understand things you never said out loud."

He looked away. Down at his hands. The cuticles chewed raw, fingers restless.

"I wasn't trying to shut you out. I just... I didn't know how to bring you in," he said, his voice barely audible.

Vaani's heart cracked—not because she was still in love with him, but because some part of her would always mourn the version of him she had waited for.

"You let me guess everything," she whispered. "You made me script the story alone."

His eyes closed briefly, like the truth had landed like glass between his ribs.

"I was scared," he admitted, voice rough. "Scared that if you saw the broken parts... you'd run."

"I didn't need you to be perfect," she said. "I just needed you to be present."

He looked up.

"I was present," he said, desperation coloring his tone. "I was—"

"No," she interrupted gently. "You were there. Not present. There's a difference."

The room fell into silence.

But it wasn't the warm silence they once shared after kisses or sleepy movie nights. This was the kind that held grief inside its breath. The kind that marked the point of no return.

"I wasn't afraid of your past, Aakash," she said, voice trembling despite her control. "I was afraid you hadn't left it."

His expression crumbled.

And still, she stood.

He reached for her instinctively—fingers brushing the empty space she had just left—but she was already rising.

"I don't want to be someone's healing phase," she said. "I wanted to be someone's beginning."

He opened his mouth. No words came.

"You were never second," he rasped.

"Then why did I feel like I was always waiting to be chosen?"

She didn't cry. Not this time. Her tears had already found their way into poems, into silences, into sleepless nights.

She just turned.

And walked.

The door didn't slam.

But the moment closed like the final page of a chapter she was no longer willing to re-edit.

The door clicked shut behind her.

Aakash remained frozen for a long time, staring at the empty space where Vaani had just stood. Her scent still lingered faintly—cinnamon and rain—but the warmth was gone. She hadn't slammed the door. She hadn't screamed. That, somehow, made it worse.

Quiet grief always hurt deeper.

He dropped to the floor beside the couch, his back pressed to the wall, knees drawn up. The cushions carried old creases—places where they had once sat together, curled in conversation, feet tangled, music floating in between them like soft confession.

He reached for his guitar.

It sat against the wall, half in shadow, strings a little out of tune, like him.

He placed it across his lap and let his fingers wander. No structure. No melody. Just sounds. Just sorrow turned into motion.

But every note felt unfinished.

The chords collapsed beneath his touch. The rhythm kept stalling. It was as though the music itself was mourning. Or resisting. Like the strings knew they couldn't carry the same weight anymore.

He stopped playing.

And for the first time in days, the silence wasn't peaceful—it was punishment.

Across campus, as the city folded into its evening hush, Vaani found herself beside Reyan on the cracked stone steps outside the English department. The sun had dipped low, casting the campus in gold and shadow. A stray cat curled near a planter. The breeze carried dust and jasmine.

They shared a quiet chai, the paper cups warm against their fingers. Neither spoke for a while. The quiet didn't demand to be filled. It simply lived between them.

Reyan glanced at her sideways. "Rough day?"

She nodded. "It feels like I'm grieving someone who's still breathing."

He didn't offer platitudes. Didn't rush to soothe.

He just let her words sit in the air, giving them space.

"Love can be like that," he said softly. "Grief in slow motion."

Vaani let out a small, hollow laugh. "You always say the worst things in the best way."

He smirked. "Maybe because I've lived the worst things."

She studied him for a long second.

His face was composed, as always. But there was something quiet and carved in his features. A sadness that didn't announce itself, but stayed. Like a watermark beneath all his calm.

"You make things feel lighter," she said suddenly, her voice low.

Reyan turned to her fully now. "I'm not here to fix you, Vaani. I don't think anyone has the right to offer that."

She looked down at her hands. The chipped nail polish. The way her fingers trembled, just a little.

"I don't need fixing," she said. "Just... room."

"And time," Reyan added.

She nodded. "And someone who doesn't walk away when I'm quiet."

He didn't say anything more. He didn't need to.

He just gently bumped his shoulder against hers, once, as if to say: I'm here. You don't have to speak to be heard.

That night, Aakash stayed awake until the sky turned the color of steel.

No new song emerged.

No apology seemed right.

He didn't know how to rewrite what had been lost. He only knew the silence she left behind was louder than any melody he could find.

Vaani reached home just as the city began to exhale.

It was that strange hour between dusk and night when everything felt suspended. The streetlights blinked on one by one like shy thoughts. A radio played somewhere faintly—an old love song from another time. The elevator in her building buzzed softly as it rose, and in that hum she found an unexpected comfort.

She entered her flat and stood for a moment in the living room, the silence hanging like fresh laundry—clean, undisturbed. Her sweater was damp from the ocean breeze, her eyes heavy not from tears but from the ache that lived in their place now.

She didn't turn on the overhead light. She didn't need to.

She made her way to her room, changed into a cotton tee, and lit the small scented candle near her window. Its flame flickered against the glass, dancing like a heartbeat that wasn't quite steady, but wasn't giving up either.

Then she sat on her bed, cross-legged, her journal resting on her lap.

She opened to a new page.

This time, there was no hesitation. No fear of the blank space.

She began to write—not a poem, not a letter. Just fragments. Truths. Sentences that didn't need to sound pretty to be real.

Today, I closed a door that had stayed open too long, letting ghosts in with every gust.

Today, I was not cruel. I was honest.

And maybe that's harder.

She paused, fingers brushing over the ink.

Outside, the wind picked up, rustling the curtains. The candle trembled.

Her phone buzzed once on the nightstand.

It wasn't Aakash.

It wasn't Reyan.

It was Meera.

Meera: *Pizza and peace tonight? My treat.*

Vaani smiled. A real one. Small, cracked at the edges—but true.

She typed back: *Give me thirty minutes. I'll bring the wine.*

She set her journal down.

Not because she was finished—but because she was finally ready to stop carrying it alone.

As she slipped on a light jacket and grabbed her bag, she caught her reflection in the mirror.

She looked different.

Not because her hair was neatly pinned or because her eyes had stopped looking tired.

But because for the first time in weeks, she didn't look like she was waiting.

She looked like she had decided.

To heal. To move. To breathe without asking for permission.

To choose herself.

And maybe, just maybe—that was the most radical kind of love there was.

Chapter Ten

Between Two Fires

The days that followed felt like walking barefoot over invisible coals—Vaani moved through them with practiced grace, but every step left its mark. Nothing exploded. No grand argument or dramatic confrontation shook the foundations of her days. But everything... stung. Quietly. Repeatedly.

Outwardly, she was thriving.

Her professors praised her insights—"elegantly argued," "exceptionally nuanced," "refreshing clarity." In class, she asked just enough questions to appear engaged, scribbled notes with mechanical precision, and always arrived on time with a highlighter tucked behind one ear like a badge of control.

Her peers noticed. Some murmured admiration. Others, curiosity. A few whispered with interest about the visiting alumnus who now often accompanied her down corridors and toward the library lawn.

Reyan Kaul. Tall. Sharp-witted. Steady as a lighthouse.

He was everywhere she was. Not in a suffocating way, but like background music that adjusted to the pace of her steps. He didn't demand anything. He just noticed. The way she twisted her ring when she was anxious. The way she reread certain lines in her notebook, underlining only when her breath hitched. The way she always paused before saying something vulnerable—waiting, perhaps, for permission.

He brought her coffee at the exact moment she began yawning into her sleeve. Extra strong. No sugar. A cinnamon stick nestled inside like a whispered reminder: *I see you.*

He quoted her. Not in flashy ways, but in quiet references—a phrase from her journal, a metaphor she had half-mumbled in passing. Like her words were dropped feathers and he was catching them mid-air before they disappeared.

Vaani appreciated him. Deeply.

But appreciation, she learned, was not the same as ache.

Because even in the softest moments—between notebook pages and gentle glances—her heart sometimes betrayed her. It wandered. Not by choice, but by muscle memory.

It drifted to undone lyrics and half-played melodies. To fingers strumming in frustration and smiles that bloomed slowly. To chai-stained shirts and boyish shrugs.

To Aakash.

She hated that. Hated how absence could still echo louder than presence.

But the truth remained: Reyan was steady.

Aakash had been fire.

One afternoon, as they packed up notes after a lecture on postmodern fragmentation, Reyan leaned casually against the sunlit edge of her desk.

"There's this place I want to take you to," he said, spinning his pen between fingers with practiced ease.

Vaani raised a brow. "Is this your attempt at postmodern flirting?"

He chuckled. "I'd be more subtle if I thought it'd work. But no—genuinely. There's a spoken word night tonight. Tiny venue. Hidden behind two bookstores in Fort. They serve cinnamon hot chocolate and play jazz before the mic opens."

She pretended to weigh her options. "You had me at cinnamon."

He grinned, his eyes lighting up with a rare kind of softness. "I had a feeling."

The venue was exactly as he described—tucked between forgotten bookshelves and the scent of vanilla tobacco. The walls were lined with polaroids of past performers, their expressions frozen mid-rhyme. Mismatched cushions dotted the floor, and strings of fairy lights dipped low across the beams like lazy constellations.

They found a spot near the window, where rain tapped gently against the glass in a syncopated rhythm. Vaani let herself relax. She hadn't realized how tightly she had been wound until her shoulders finally began to fall.

People took turns at the mic—some trembling, some practiced. Their poems were messy and tender. About breakups. About politics. About mothers who never said "I love you" but always cut the fruit just right.

Then Reyan stood up.

He didn't announce himself with flair. No dramatic voice or over-rehearsed swagger. He just walked to the mic, adjusted it gently, and began.

His poem was about dreams.

Not the inspirational kind, but the complicated ones. The ones that outgrow you, or the ones you outgrow. About versions of self that no longer fit. About standing in a place you once called home and realizing it doesn't recognize you anymore.

His voice didn't rise. It lowered.

It pulled the room in like gravity, each pause heavier than the words themselves.

Vaani watched, entranced.

Not because he was dazzling. But because he was *true*. Every word he said lived first in him, and then in the space between.

She clapped with everyone else.

But something inside her shifted. Just slightly.

A pang.

A song she hadn't thought about in days rose in her chest.

A boy with tired eyes and calloused fingers.

Not Reyan.

Aakash.

Not because Reyan wasn't enough.

But because memory didn't ask permission.

Later, they sat by a fogged-up window, steam curling from chipped mugs of cinnamon hot chocolate. Outside, the world had blurred—rain-slick pavements shimmered with streetlight reflections, the occasional car carving through puddles with a hiss. But inside the café, the world was warm, dim, safe.

Vaani traced the rim of her mug with one finger, watching the swirl of chocolate and cream settle into stillness.

"You're not really here," Reyan said quietly.

It wasn't an accusation. Just an observation. Soft and without edges.

Vaani looked up.

Her first instinct was to deny it—to pull on the old armor of I'm fine, I'm just tired. But Reyan's gaze held hers, unflinching. Not demanding. Just open.

"I'm trying to be," she admitted.

He nodded, his thumb resting against the curve of his mug. He didn't fill the silence. He waited.

Finally, she exhaled, her breath fogging the window beside them.

"It's not that I'm stuck in the past," she said, barely above a whisper. "It's just... I don't know how to make room for the present when the past hasn't stopped echoing."

Reyan leaned slightly closer, enough that his voice felt like warmth but not pressure.

"I don't need all of you, Vaani," he said. "Not yet. Maybe not ever. I just need honesty. Am I standing somewhere that still belongs to someone else?"

She swallowed hard. The question hit somewhere deep. Not because it was unfair, but because it was fairer than most people ever dared to be.

She looked down at her hands.

"It's not about space," she murmured. "It's about time. I'm somewhere between letting go and not knowing how."

Reyan nodded. No surprise. No disappointment.

"Then let me be here," he said. "Not to replace. Not to erase. Just… to be."

She looked at him—really looked.

His patience. His steadiness. The quiet knowing in his eyes.

"You make it sound easy," she said, a small, tired smile playing at her lips.

"It's not," he replied gently. "But you're worth the hard parts."

She blinked at that—because it didn't hurt. It didn't scare her. It didn't make her feel like she owed him something.

For the first time in weeks, someone wanted her just as she was—incomplete, honest, healing.

And for the first time, she didn't feel like she had to apologize for it.

The next morning rose without ceremony.

No dramatic shift in the sky. Just soft grey clouds pulling across the skyline, the city stretching its limbs as rickshaws honked half-heartedly and chai stalls hissed to life.

Vaani moved through the day like someone brushing her fingertips along the fabric of a dream—half-asleep but not sleepwalking.

Class. Notes. Canteen banter. A pop quiz. A poem read out loud in the corridor by an overenthusiastic literature student. Life, stubborn and uninterrupted.

At the end of the day, she stopped by the grocery store to pick up lemons and turmeric—a mundane task she usually delegated to Sunday afternoons. But today, the ordinariness of it grounded her.

She walked slowly through the aisles, her thoughts blissfully blank.

Until she turned the corner.

And everything rushed back.

There, standing near the entrance with a half-squashed loaf of bread in one hand and a plastic bag in the other, was **Aakash**.

The fluorescent lights above him buzzed slightly. A fan spun uselessly overhead. The smell of wet cardboard and green chilies lingered in the air.

But she didn't notice any of it.

Only him.

And he saw her.

Of course he did.

Their eyes met across baskets of produce and checkout queues, and for a second, the entire world seemed to mute itself.

"Hey," he said, stepping forward. His voice was hoarse, like it hadn't been used for too long—or like it had been used too much in his own head.

"Hey," she replied, softer. Measured.

The rain outside had just begun to fall, a soft, pattering drizzle against the glass. The sky turned a little darker.

Aakash fumbled with the bread in his hand, his posture unsure for the first time in a long while.

"How've you been?" he asked, as if the question wasn't too small to hold everything they'd been through.

"Busy," she said. "You?"

"Trying," he admitted, with a crooked smile that didn't reach his eyes. "I heard about the poetry night. Reyan read something beautiful."

Her heart gave a small jolt.

"You were there?" she asked, surprised.

He shook his head. "Someone sent me a video."

A beat passed. The sound of a child crying in aisle three filtered in. A woman at the counter argued about a wrong price tag. Life pulsed around them, uncaring.

"I've been writing again," Aakash said. "About us. About everything I never said."

Vaani gripped the lemons in her hand a little tighter. Their waxy skin pressed into her palm like a grounding spell.

"I don't know what I'm supposed to feel right now," she said.

"You don't have to feel anything," Aakash murmured. "I just needed you to know—I never stopped choosing you. I just forgot how to show it."

There it was.

Too late. Too early. Too raw.

She blinked back tears, but didn't let them fall.

She shook her head slowly. Stepped back.

"I need time, Aakash," she said gently. "I'm tired of healing from people who are still bleeding on me."

He didn't follow.

Didn't plead.

He just stood there, heartbreak plain on his face. Shoulders heavy. Mouth pressed shut.

And for once, she didn't wish he would chase her.

She turned.

And walked out into the rain.

The sky outside had shifted to a moody charcoal by the time she made it home.

Vaani dropped the lemons and turmeric on the kitchen counter with a soft thud, slipped off her sandals, and padded barefoot into her room. The rain had followed her back—not loudly, not violently. Just the kind that tapped gently at the windows like a memory asking to be let in.

She stood by the window for a long time, forehead against the glass, watching the droplets race each other to the sill.

What had she expected from seeing Aakash again?

Closure? No. That was too neat a word for what they had lived.

Maybe clarity. But even that was slippery.

His words had clung to her—not just the *I never stopped choosing you* but the quiet ache behind them. That pain... it was real. It mirrored hers. But pain, she was learning, wasn't a currency she was willing to trade anymore. Not even for love.

She glanced at her desk.

Reyan's napkin note was still there—folded once, scribbled in his quick, slanted writing. She unfolded it now, smoothing the creases.

Some people hold fire. Others hold the space around it.

She read it twice. Then again.

It wasn't a grand confession. It was a recognition. A kind of truth she hadn't been able to name herself.

Aakash had been fire.

Reyan had been space.

And maybe, right now, what she needed most was neither.

Maybe she just needed her own breath. Her own pace.

Vaani grabbed her shawl and stepped back into the night.

The sea face greeted her like it always did—with no questions, no conditions.

The pavement glistened under the streetlamps. Waves rolled in quietly, rhythmic and unbothered by human heartbreak. Couples huddled close on benches. Dogs padded by, chasing shadows. A tea vendor poured from his kettle, steam rising like incense into the evening.

She didn't stop.

She didn't sit at the usual bench, the one where first kisses and shared silences once lingered. She didn't retrace the path of nostalgia.

She just walked.

Let the wind mess her hair. Let the salt kiss her skin. Let the rain touch her without apology.

And as she walked, something began to loosen. Not dramatically. Not all at once. But piece by piece.

The guilt of not choosing Aakash.

The pressure of making Reyan's steadiness worth it.

The ache of trying to be okay for everyone except herself.

She let it all fall behind her like breadcrumbs she no longer intended to follow.

Tonight, she wasn't suspended between two fires.

She was stepping out of the flame.

Not because she had healed completely but because she had finally chosen to walk forward even with the burn.

Chapter Eleven

Quiet Spaces, Quieter Hearts

The city, ever indifferent, moved forward.

Trains roared across their tracks like restless storytellers, urgent and unfiltered. Vendors barked their familiar calls—"Cutting chai! Vada pav!"—their voices blurring with the honks and squeals of traffic. The Arabian Sea sang lullabies only the wind seemed to understand. Life, vibrant and chaotic, continued its dance, unconcerned with hearts paused mid-beat.

Mumbai didn't stop for heartbreak. It simply offered more noise to drown it in.

Vaani noticed this from her new sanctuary—a shaded bench beneath the sprawling banyan tree tucked behind the sociology department. The world here was gentler. The roots twisted like old secrets into the ground, the rustling leaves a soft chorus that muted the city's din. This little space had no expectations. No reminders of music or kisses or storms.

Just silence. And for now, that felt like mercy.

She came here most afternoons now, her faded tote stuffed with underlined novels and a notebook whose pages had grown more thoughtful, less desperate. Her fingers still wrote about longing, but the lines no longer bled. They breathed.

Sometimes Reyan would find her there.

He never startled her. Never interrupted. He'd arrive with a quiet rhythm, his footsteps slow, measured, carrying two paper cups of tea that always steamed just right.

He never assumed.

He always asked, "Room for one more?"

And she'd nod.

It was easy with him. The way he respected silence without fearing it. He didn't try to distract her with plans or drag her out of her moods with forced laughter. He simply... stayed.

"Did you know Neruda wrote letters to the moon?" he asked one day, his voice barely above the rustle of leaves.

She looked up from her book, curious. "Really?"

Reyan smiled, tucking a loose page into his journal. "Not literally. But he once said that longing is like moonlight—quiet, unavoidable, and always slipping through the cracks."

Vaani smiled faintly. "Sounds like a man who knew his metaphors."

He chuckled. "Or his heartbreaks."

Sometimes they'd read side by side. Other times, they'd trade lines—poems, passages, memories. Once, she played him a scratchy ghazal from her father's old collection. He listened all the way through, his eyes closed, head nodding to the rhythm.

No commentary. No performance. Just presence.

It was… kind.

But even in this slow safety, shadows stirred.

Every now and then, a memory of Aakash would rise like a tide she hadn't braced for—a sudden scent of monsoon-soaked streets, the faint echo of a guitar chord from a nearby hostel room, or the way a chai cup's rim curved just like the ones he always bought. Her fingers would twitch toward the edge of her notebook. Her thoughts would drift—uninvited, but not entirely unwelcome.

She didn't cry anymore when he came to mind.

But she didn't smile either.

Across the city, in a rented room that had once felt warmer with her laughter lingering in its corners, **Aakash** was unlearning old patterns.

The days no longer blurred into chords or apologies.

He rose early now—not to write songs, but to walk.

Long, shapeless walks through the tangled lanes of Fort, down the Bandra promenade, across quiet corners of Marine Drive where no one asked for his name. His guitar, once an appendage, now rested against the wall, untouched for days at a time. Not abandoned—just no longer desperate.

He wasn't composing verses about her anymore.

Instead, he was listening to the world again. Watching. Absorbing.

A tea vendor's radio crackled with an old Kishore Kumar ballad one morning, and Aakash stood there, unmoving, letting the nostalgia wash over him. He bought a cup. Burnt his tongue and smiled at the sting.

At night, he filled journals with things he didn't have to show anyone.

Not lyrics. Not love letters.

Just... truths.

Some scribbled in haste:

- "She wasn't the silence. I was."

Some written slowly, deliberately:

- "She deserved songs that didn't have to earn their chorus."

Others were barely legible beneath ink smudges and tea stains:

- "Some love isn't lost. It just rests in a room you don't walk into anymore."

He pinned them to the wall. Not as reminders of failure. But as markers of movement. He was learning. Softly. Stubbornly. Alone.

There were still moments when grief knelt on his chest—a sudden flash of her laugh echoing in the marketplace, the scent of cinnamon wafting from a café. But he didn't run toward those moments anymore. He let them pass.

He even tried writing again—just once.

A song with no title, no chorus. Just a verse:

If I see you again in a crowd or a storm,

I won't ask you to stay,

But I'll thank you for showing me

What it meant to want to.

And he left it at that.

Their paths crossed again—of course they did. Mumbai wasn't big enough to hide from coincidence.

It was a **Saturday afternoon**. A rare sunbeam spilled across Colaba Causeway, the air thick with the scent of damp cloth and old ink.

The bookstore—**their bookstore**—was hosting a clearance sale.

Aakash had wandered in, drawn by instinct more than intention. The fiction aisle smelled like yellowed paperbacks and forgotten margins. The poetry section sagged under the weight of emotions others had already written for him.

He was flipping through a Neruda collection when he saw her.

Vaani.

She stood beneath a beam of dusty light, her fingertips brushing the spine of a Murakami novel. She looked exactly the same. And nothing like before.

He didn't panic. He didn't prepare a monologue.

He simply walked forward.

She sensed him before she saw him. When she turned, their eyes met. Familiar. Worn. Softened by everything unsaid.

Neither of them broke.

"Hey," she said. Barely above the shuffle of old pages.

"Hey," he replied.

There was no tremble. No lingering ache. Just recognition. Just... closure, in its gentlest form.

Her fingers still rested on the book. He held a poetry anthology like it might spill memories if he clutched it too tightly.

"You still read Neruda," she said.

"You still wear that ring," he nodded, gesturing to the silver band on her index finger—the one she used to fiddle with when nervous.

She glanced down. Smiled faintly. "Some habits don't leave."

"No," he said. "They just change shape."

They didn't hug. Didn't exchange numbers. Didn't say goodbye.

They just stood for a breath longer, the bookstore humming quietly around them.

Then they turned—him to the counter, her to the staircase.

Opposite directions.

But—and this mattered—it didn't feel like breaking.

It didn't feel like regret.

It felt like two people who had loved each other once. Deeply. Chaotically. Briefly.

And now, were learning how to love themselves.

Chapter Twelve

When the Lights Flickered

It happened on a Thursday—the kind that offered lullabies in its breeze. The clouds hung low, indifferent yet watchful, and the city, for once, seemed to exhale. There was no warning. No flicker to prepare her. Just—darkness. Sudden, absolute, and oddly intimate.

Vaani sat at her desk, one leg curled under her, her laptop screen glowing faintly with half-formed thoughts. Her coffee had gone cold long ago. It tasted of regret now—of chapters she didn't want to revisit, of pauses she hadn't chosen. Her pen was uncapped, but the words weren't coming. They hadn't, for days.

When the power cut, it took her heartbeat with it for a moment.

The ceiling fan wheezed once before stilling. The screen blinked twice—then surrendered to the night. A silence, thick and unexpected, settled into the room. The kind of silence that doesn't just fill a space—it reclaims it.

She didn't move at first.

Not out of fear, but because it felt as though the universe had paused just for her. As if the world wanted to give her a moment to breathe. To listen.

Her hand reached for her phone. A flicker. No signal. No Wi-Fi. No pending messages. Nothing to reach out to, no one waiting at the other end.

The kind of blackout Mumbai rarely had anymore. It felt almost... intentional. Like the city had chosen stillness over chaos for a night.

Somewhere in the distance, a pressure cooker whistled—once, sharply—then nothing. Dogs barked, briefly, before being swallowed by the hush. Vaani stepped into the kitchen, the coolness of the tiles grounding her. She struck a match.

The flame caught with a hiss.

She lit a candle and stood there, just holding it— watching how the light made the walls sway, how her own shadow shivered on the ceiling. The flame was unsteady, but it didn't die. It reminded her of something she couldn't name.

The porch called to her next.

The breeze had shifted, damp with monsoon hints. The smell of wet earth and electricity clung to the night like perfume on an old scarf. And then, as she stepped outside, she saw it.

Across the street—**a glow**.

Aakash.

Sitting by his window, guitar in his lap, his face lit with a single flickering candle. The moment didn't feel real. It felt... rehearsed by the universe. Like the city had orchestrated this power cut not to inconvenience, but to nudge.

To remind them.

Their eyes met. Not suddenly, but slowly—as though their gaze had been waiting for a crack in time to realign.

She didn't look away.

Aakash didn't move at first.

He sat there, still, the guitar resting against his knee, one hand caught mid-air as if frozen mid-thought. The candlelight softened him—turned the edges of his face to something almost unreal. He looked less like the boy she had walked away from, and more like the boy she had once fallen into.

Then, he blinked.

Lifted his hand—slowly, cautiously.

A wave. Just that.

Vaani's breath caught in her chest. The world around her held its breath too. She didn't wave back right away. She let the air between them stretch. Let the memory of silence press gently against her ribs.

And then, with the smallest tilt of her wrist, she lifted her hand. An echo of his. A call across the canyon of everything that had gone unspoken.

Aakash's lips curved—not into a smile, exactly. But into something softer. Grateful. He adjusted his guitar slightly, his fingers settling on the strings. A moment passed. Then another.

Then—**he strummed**.

One chord.

Then another.

The sound was thin, carried across the damp air like a secret whispered from one soul to another. The melody was fragile, unsteady. But it was alive. And familiar.

Vaani's chest tightened.

She knew that song.

The one he had hummed under his breath the night they'd danced in her room, laughing over spilt chai and poetry lines. The one he never finished. The one he said didn't need words, because it was "meant to be felt."

She hadn't heard it since before the silence. Since before they'd become ghosts in each other's lives.

Now, under candlelight and clouded skies, **he was playing it again.**

Her feet moved before her mind caught up.

Barefoot, candle in hand, she stepped off the porch. The wax trickled down the side of her palm, unnoticed. The road was slick from a day of off-and-on drizzle, but she didn't care. Her steps were quiet, certain. The kind you take when the ache of standing still becomes too loud to bear.

Each window she passed flickered with candlelight. It felt like walking through someone else's dream.

Aakash stood as she approached.

He hadn't changed. And yet—he had. The tiredness in his shoulders was new. So was the hope in his eyes.

His guitar lay forgotten on the chair behind him now. He stepped out onto his own porch, mirroring her. They stood like that—just across from one another. Two silhouettes caught between memory and something unnamed.

"You came," he said, his voice barely above the hush of the wind.

"I don't know why," she replied honestly. "But I couldn't sit still."

His throat worked through a swallow. "I wasn't sure you'd even look."

"I didn't think I would either."

He stepped forward, then paused—one foot on the stair, the other in uncertainty.

"I never stopped writing," he said.

Her heart flinched. "I never stopped reading."

The words hung between them, delicate and raw.

He reached out his hand—not to take hers, but just to offer it. Open. Empty. Willing.

"I can't promise I've figured everything out," he said. "But I can promise I won't disappear again. Not like that."

Vaani looked at his hand, then up at his face. She saw the boy who once kissed her under streetlamps. Who once whispered Neruda into her collarbone. Who once broke her by doing nothing at all.

She stepped forward. Slowly.

Her fingers touched his. Not to hold. Just to say, *I'm here. I remember.*

Then, without a word, she rested her forehead against his shoulder.

He didn't move. Just breathed her in. His hand hovered near her back, unsure. Waiting.

"You smell like wax and rain," he murmured. A half-laugh, half-sigh.

"You smell like bad decisions and nostalgia," she whispered back, and for the first time in weeks, they both smiled.

There were no apologies.

No rehearsed speeches.

No sudden declarations.

Just silence. And warmth. And flickering light.

Above them, the clouds rolled on. The blackout remained. The city stayed hushed.

But there, in the middle of a candlelit street, **something returned**.

Not like a firework.

Not like a flood.

But like an ember—small, flickering, refusing to go out.

A beginning. Or maybe, a remembering.

Chapter Thirteen

Salt and Flame

The next morning, sunlight streamed through Colaba's narrow lanes, spilling across balconies, puddles, and the delicate thresholds of quiet homes. In Vaani's room, dust particles danced lazily in the golden beams filtering through the sheer curtains. The warm glow did little to soothe the tension curled up inside her. Candlelight had faded, and in its place stood morning's blunt truth—everything looked different in daylight.

She found herself staring out the window, watching Aakash move about in his kitchen. From this distance, he looked like a memory. Familiar. Distant. Not quite hers.

They hadn't spoken since the blackout. No calls. No messages. Just that moment beneath the broken streetlight.

And now, in the harsh light of morning, she wasn't sure what it had meant.

She wanted to believe the silence that followed was comforting, respectful. But beneath that hope churned unease. That moment, as tender as it was, had not untangled the knots in her chest. It had merely dimmed them.

Two days passed. She didn't write. She barely slept. The world resumed, but she stayed inside her head, stuck between what had been felt and what had been said.

It was a Tuesday afternoon when Vaani found herself seated on the shaded patio of the college café with Reyan. They were reviewing edits for the upcoming campus journal. Papers were strewn across the table, highlighters tucked behind ears, and coffee mugs leaving circular imprints like timestamps on the wood.

Reyan was telling her a story about a misprinted poem in his college magazine. "They printed my 'void' piece and misspelled the title as 'vapid.' My mother called to ask if I'd finally run out of words," he said with a grin.

Vaani laughed. "Maybe it's poetic justice. 'Vapid void' sounds like a decent band name."

He chuckled, shaking his head. "Only if you're the lead singer."

She was about to retort when her gaze lifted—drawn by instinct—and landed on Aakash, standing near the café's entrance. His hair was tousled, and he looked slightly breathless, as if he hadn't intended to find her here but now couldn't walk away.

Their eyes locked.

His posture stiffened. His smile—half-formed—dissolved.

He walked toward them.

"Hey," he said, tone clipped but not cold. "Didn't expect to see you both here."

Vaani's smile faltered into something practiced. "We're finalizing the piece for the journal."

Reyan, always composed, extended politeness. "Want to join us?"

Aakash glanced at the table—the drafts, the closeness—and then at Vaani. "No, I wouldn't want to interrupt something that looks so... involved."

The tension settled like mist.

Reyan, sensing the shift, stood. "I'll grab us more coffee. Same as usual?"

Vaani nodded. Her throat was tight.

As Reyan stepped away, Aakash sat down in the seat he left.

"You said you needed time," he said, voice low.

"I still do," she replied, her tone careful.

"But this?" He gestured toward the space Reyan had just left. "Is this what you meant by time?"

She stared at him. "You don't get to decide what my time looks like."

"I'm not trying to decide. I'm just..." He sighed, dragging a hand through his hair. "I'm trying to understand how we go from standing in the dark together to this daylight... replacement."

"That night meant something," she said quietly. "But it didn't mean a reset. It wasn't an undo button."

Aakash's expression hardened. "So that's it? You and him?"

Her eyes flared. "There is no 'me and him.' But there isn't a 'you and me' either. Not when I had to teach you how to show up."

"I was figuring myself out!"

"And I was standing there, every day, waiting for the figuring to end!"

He leaned in, the mask cracking. "I was fighting for us—writing, remembering, walking through every place we once went, thinking you might still feel something."

Vaani's voice dropped to a whisper. "I did. I do. But it's buried under every silence you gave me when I needed words."

"I wasn't silent to hurt you—"

"But you still did," she cut in. "Reyan listens. That's all. He doesn't ask for more than I can give. He doesn't flinch when I fall apart."

"And that's enough?" Aakash asked, bitterness coloring his voice.

"It's not about enough," she replied. "It's about being seen. Consistently. Fully. Not only when guilt arrives."

He stared at her. "You said you still needed time. Now it feels like you just needed someone new."

She looked down at the table, then back at him. Her voice trembled but didn't break. "At least he reads what I write."

It landed like glass between them.

Aakash stood abruptly. "I thought that night meant something."

"It did," she said. "But not everything that means something lasts."

He looked at her like he was memorizing her. Not as a lover, but as someone he was about to lose forever.

"I loved you," he said. "Maybe I still do."

"I know," she whispered. "I just wish you had loved me right."

He didn't say another word. He turned and walked away.

She sat still, chest tight, staring at the drafts on the table like they could somehow rewrite what had just happened.

Reyan returned, quiet.

"Everything alright?" he asked.

She took the coffee cup, holding it with both hands like it might steady her. "No. But I'll pretend until it is."

He didn't press. He just brushed his fingers against hers. No questions. No demands.

Outside, the wind rustled through the trees, scattering dust and dry leaves across the pavement.

Because not every reawakening leads to peace.

Some light fires.

Chapter Fourteen

After the Burn

Time didn't stop after the café confrontation. It simply moved differently—slower, more cautiously. Like the city itself knew that something delicate had fractured between two people who once lit it up with glances and verses.

The silence that settled after that day wasn't empty. It was filled with the weight of things unsaid, and heavier still with the memory of everything that had been spoken—too fast, too raw, too final.

Vaani withdrew into the rhythm of academics and responsibilities. She poured herself into editing Reyan's poetry for the campus journal. Her eyes traced lines with mechanical precision, but her heart wasn't in it. After hours in the library, she stayed back to shelve books or pretend to be working while her mind wandered to conversations that had no conclusions.

She began waking early. At dawn, when Colaba was still stretching into consciousness, she'd walk alone through the quiet lanes. Past shuttered bakeries and newspaper stacks, she let her breath align with the city's slow awakening. It made her feel invisible in the best possible way.

But she avoided certain routes—like the turn past the milkshake stall, or the garden bench near the amphitheater. Spaces that had once echoed with laughter now felt too loud in memory.

She didn't cry.

She didn't write.

Her notebook lay closed at the corner of her desk, a relic of the girl she had been when she thought love could be stitched back together with one more verse.

At night, sleep came in fragments. She would stare at the ceiling, replaying their last argument. His eyes, filled with accusation. Her voice, strained with restraint. The subtle tremble in her hands as she said, "I just wish you had loved me right."

She hated herself for wanting him to reach out. But she hated the silence more.

Aakash, too, had become a version of silence.

He stayed home. Skipped his gigs. Stopped replying to group chats. His guitar sat untouched, covered in a soft film of dust, like a shrine to a feeling he could no longer access.

For someone who had once turned everything into music, the quiet was deafening.

He cooked without tasting. Walked around the house without noticing the time. Every now and then, he'd open the notebook that held his half-written songs. He'd sit, pen in hand, and stare.

Once, he managed a single line:

"You loved me like fire, and I watched it burn from across the street."

Then nothing.

He missed her. Not the version he had idealized, not the version who laughed at his lyrics—but the real her. The sharp edges. The quiet fears. The girl who saw through his walls even when he pretended not to have any.

And he hated how much he missed being seen.

Colaba moved on. As it always did. The chai stalls stayed crowded. Rickshaws honked at random. Laughter spilled out of classrooms. Festivals came and went, dressing the streets in colors that felt more insistent than they used to.

And somewhere in the middle of that chaos, Vaani and Aakash learned to live around each other.

They didn't speak. They didn't cross paths—not really.

But the city had its own way of scripting reunions.

One afternoon, as Vaani was leaving the stationery shop, a sudden gust of wind sent pages from her folder flying. She bent to gather them just as a pair of familiar sneakers stepped into view.

She looked up. Aakash was already holding out the last page.

Their fingers brushed.

She stood, brushing her hair behind her ear.

He handed her the page. "You dropped this."

"Thanks," she said, voice quiet.

They stood there for a moment, unsure of the rules. The silence stretched.

"How have you been?" he asked, finally.

She hesitated. "Trying. You?"

"Same," he said. "Trying... and failing most days."

She let out a small breath. "Yeah. Some days feel like they're stuck on repeat."

There was a pause. He looked like he had more to say. She looked like she wouldn't stop him if he did.

"I've been thinking about that night," he said. "The blackout. The candlelight. What it felt like to stand next to you again."

She didn't answer right away. Then, "Me too. It felt... fleeting."

"I wanted to say something. That night. But I didn't want to ruin the silence."

"And now?"

He offered a half-smile. "Now, I don't know if I'm allowed to speak."

"You are," she said softly. "But I don't know if I'm ready to listen."

She glanced at the time. "I should get going."

He nodded. "Of course."

She turned to leave.

But paused.

"Aakash."

He looked up.

She didn't say anything else. Just offered a small, tired smile.

And he returned it.

No promises. No rewrites.

Just… acknowledgment.

They passed each other again a week later. This time near the old bookstore where they had once stood between poetry and possibility.

No wave.

No words.

Just a glance.

A glance that held all the heat of their old arguments and all the cold of their quiet exits.

And yet…

Beneath it all, something flickered.

Not love. Not yet.

But the possibility of understanding.

Sometimes, after the fire dies, there's no rush to rebuild.

You stay in the ash for a while… and learn to breathe again.

Chapter Fifteen

A Quiet Return

A few weeks passed.

Life didn't pause for heartbreak. It carried on like the sea—relentless, unbothered, washing over everything in its path.

While Vaani threw herself into her final semester projects, organizing group presentations and revising thesis drafts, Reyan's life moved into a new orbit. He had been selected to lead a national writing workshop, a prestigious traveling assignment that would take him across cities. The news was met with celebration from the campus literary circle, and for a while, it became the most talked-about headline in Vaani's world.

They celebrated one last time before his departure. The café buzzed with clinking glasses, overused toasts, and quiet moments laced with nostalgia. Reyan stood with a mug of chai in hand, the foam already sinking into his fingers. "To pages turned, poems still unwritten, and people who walked us through both," he said, raising his glass with an easy smile.

Vaani smiled back, warm but distant. She clapped, toasted, laughed when expected. But inside, something had stilled. As Reyan left, he squeezed her hand a little longer than necessary. She didn't say much. She didn't need to. In his absence, the air around her felt lighter. Not because he had burdened her—but because without the steadiness of his gaze, there was suddenly more room to feel things she hadn't dared to while he was around.

In his absence, the air around her felt lighter. Not because he had burdened her—but because without the steadiness of his gaze, there was suddenly more room to feel things she hadn't dared to while he was around. And in that stillness, silence didn't punish—it questioned. Gently. Persistently.

One Sunday morning, Vaani left her apartment without a plan. The city was calm—the kind of calm only Sunday mornings slipped under your skin. No rickshaw horns. No vendor calls. Just a slower sky, and streets that seemed to breathe softer. Colaba's lanes wore a lazy, sun-washed look. Shops were still shuttered, and the smell of roasted peanuts curled through the air like memory. She walked slowly, without music, without distraction.

Eventually, she found herself at the promenade. It greeted her like an old diary page—weathered, personal. She walked along the edge, her hand trailing the cold stone ledge until she reached the bench. *Their* bench.

The wood was slightly warm from the sun. She sat and pulled her scarf tighter around her shoulders. In front of her, the sea moved with its usual indifference. Behind her, the city breathed on.

She closed her eyes.

And when she opened them, he was there.

Aakash.

He stood a few feet away, his figure still familiar. A little more tired, a little more quiet. His hands were buried in his pockets, and his mouth pressed into a nervous line.

"I didn't mean to interrupt," he said, voice uncertain.

"You didn't," Vaani replied softly, patting the space beside her.

He hesitated, then walked over and sat down. Careful not to let their shoulders touch. Close enough to feel the pull. Far enough to honor the wound.

They watched the sea together.

"I wasn't planning to come here today," Aakash said. "It just... happened."

Vaani glanced at him. "Most important things do."

He offered a small smile, more rueful than happy. "I've been writing again."

She turned back to the horizon. "That's good. Writing is healing. Even when it hurts."

He nodded. "This time it's different. I'm not trying to rhyme regrets or lace them in metaphor. I'm just writing what I should've said when it mattered."

Vaani didn't answer immediately.

He went on. "I kept trying to write you an apology. But everything sounded like I was defending myself."

"You don't need to," she said. "Not anymore. Apologies are like keys. They only work when the other person still wants to open the door."

He turned to her. "Do you?"

She looked at him, long and quiet. "I think I want to rebuild the house before I open the door again."

He chuckled lightly, then shook his head. "You always were better at metaphors."

A moment passed.

"I loved you in pieces," Aakash said, almost to himself. "I didn't realize how unfair that was until I saw how much you had to break just to hold me together."

Vaani blinked slowly. "And I waited for you to offer something whole, without realizing you hadn't yet found those pieces yourself."

He sighed. "I'm sorry, Vaani. For all the times I made you feel like you were waiting for something that never came."

She reached into her bag.

Her journal had dust at the edges, the spine creased, pages marked with starts and stops. She flipped it open, scanned through, then tore out a single sheet. She folded it once, then again, and handed it to him.

He opened it slowly.

Maybe we're not what we were. Maybe we never will be. But I still hope you find peace In the version of me That loved you anyway.

Aakash held the page like it was fragile. Like it might disappear if he breathed too hard.

His voice caught. "This... is the most beautiful thing you've ever given me."

"It's not a gift," she said. "It's a release."

He nodded. Then whispered, "It still means more than you know."

They didn't say much else.

But they didn't have to.

The sea moved. The wind rustled. Somewhere, a child laughed. The world, unbothered by two people remembering how to forgive.

No grand declarations. No second-chance kiss.

Just a beginning.

Or maybe, the end of something that needed to end before anything else could begin.

Not love. Not yet.

But the slow, deliberate thaw of something that refused to die.

The Echo of Almost

It began with coffee.

Not the kind passed across counters in bustling cafes, scrawled with misspelled names and served with obligatory smiles. No, this coffee was different. It came in a steel flask wrapped in a navy-blue kitchen towel, held tight in Aakash's trembling hands as he stood outside Vaani's apartment just as the sun dipped below the Mumbai skyline, casting long shadows across Colaba's quiet lanes. He also held two mismatched ceramic mugs—one with a fading cartoon cat, the other chipped at the rim.

He hadn't called. He hadn't texted.

He just... showed up.

When Vaani opened the door, she looked like she had been reading. A pencil was tucked behind one ear, and the collar of her loose sweatshirt hung off one shoulder. Her expression, however, was unreadable—not surprised, not angry, but caught somewhere between curiosity and cautiousness.

"I didn't want to text," Aakash said, lifting the flask slightly. "Some conversations deserve steam and silence."

A slow blink. Then a dry smile. "That's a new line. You rehearse that on the way here?"

He chuckled nervously. "Twice. Third time felt honest."

She leaned against the doorframe, arms crossed. The air between them was thick with all the things they had never managed to say.

Then, without another word, she stepped aside.

He entered slowly, like stepping into a dream you're afraid you might ruin just by breathing. The flat still smelled faintly of jasmine and old books. There was a pile of laundry half-folded on the edge of the bed and a playlist humming quietly from her speaker—a song that neither belonged to joy nor sorrow.

They settled on the floor, backs against the bed, legs crossed like children trading secrets. The light from her desk lamp bathed them in a syrupy glow, softening the edges of everything—their words, their regrets, their distance.

Aakash unscrewed the flask and poured the steaming coffee into the mismatched mugs. Their fingers brushed as they passed them along, and though it lasted less than a second, it stretched across memory like a bridge suspended in mist.

"I still sleep on the right side of the bed," he murmured after a long sip.

Vaani turned to him, eyebrows raised. "Even when you're alone?"

He nodded, looking somewhere beyond the room. "Habit. Hope. I don't know."

She sipped in silence.

The coffee was strong, just the way she liked it. It tasted of familiarity. Of memories too old to change but too dear to discard. Of fireflies and silence and the messes between.

She leaned gently against his shoulder, tentative but sure. He didn't flinch. He stayed.

They sat like that for a long time.

Not talking. Not touching beyond what had already been allowed. Just breathing together in the same rhythm—the kind of rhythm that takes weeks to rebuild and seconds to lose.

When Vaani finally spoke, it was barely above a whisper.

"I don't know what this is."

"Neither do I," Aakash replied.

She tilted her head, resting her cheek more fully on his shoulder. "But it feels real."

"It does."

She paused. "Are we being foolish?"

He looked down at her, eyes soft. "Maybe. But it's our kind of foolish."

She closed her eyes.

That night, there were no kisses, no confessions, no attempts to undo what had already been done. But in the stillness, something shifted. A layer peeled back. A wound inhaled.

Outside, the city went on as it always did—oblivious to two people trying to navigate the echo of what they had almost been.

And in that quiet room, lit by lamplight and shadowed by memory, they sat side by side with mugs in hand and hearts cautiously open, beginning again without calling it a beginning.

Not a second chance. Not yet.

Just the possibility of one.

In the days that followed, the world around them remained unchanged—loud traffic, damp balconies, borrowed umbrellas—but something had shifted between Aakash and Vaani. Not drastically. Not in grand gestures. But in the softness of how they looked at each other again. In the accidental texts that no longer felt like accidents. In the way they chose to walk the same side of the road.

They didn't define it. They didn't even talk about it. They just... kept showing up.

One afternoon, under the banyan tree that had once been her escape, Vaani handed him a folded page from her journal. No explanation.

He read it slowly. Five lines. A poem that began with silence and ended with breath.

"Do I get to keep this?" he asked.

She nodded.

That weekend, he brought his guitar. Played a melody for her that had no name but felt like home. She didn't cry. She didn't clap. She just listened, eyes closed, head tilted, as if memorizing every note.

They built new rituals. Morning chai from her favorite Irani stall. Sunday walks near the broken lighthouse. Quiet afternoons at the bookstore, arguing over editions. They never spoke of forever. But they spoke of maybe. Of someday.

Then, on a dull Tuesday afternoon, the 'maybe' cracked.

Reyan returned.

No warning. Just a messenger bag, worn sneakers, and a presence that once steadied her.

He saw them first—Vaani and Aakash at the campus gate. She laughed, brushing hair from her face. Aakash touched her shoulder lightly. It wasn't dramatic. But it was intimate. Familiar.

Reyan didn't interrupt. He just walked away.

Later that night, her phone buzzed.

Reyan: *Guess I was never really in the running, huh?*

Then another.

Reyan: *Thanks for the honesty you never gave me.*

She stared at the screen.

She typed.

Deleted.

Typed again.

But nothing felt right.

Eventually, she powered off the phone.

The guilt came slow, like smoke through a locked room. She hadn't cheated. She hadn't lied. But she had lingered too long between two doors, and now both frames felt charred.

Aakash noticed.

"You're quieter," he said one evening as they sat in her room, feet tangled under a shared blanket.

"I feel like I broke something," she replied. "Not between us. Just... something good."

"Maybe you did," he said gently. "But it wasn't because you meant to."

She looked at him, tears brimming. "I just didn't expect to hurt someone else while trying to heal myself."

He didn't speak for a while. Then, "We've all done that. Some people bleed on the people who never cut them."

She nodded slowly. "I don't want to be that person."

"Then don't run. Stay. Learn. Try."

But a part of her had already begun to retreat.

They met at the sea face two days later. No one else. No texts sent before. Just instinct.

She arrived first. He followed ten minutes later, carrying nothing but a pen tucked behind his ear.

"I wrote you something," he said, sitting beside her.

She looked at him, unsure.

"But I won't read it. Not unless you ask."

She smiled sadly. "Maybe one day."

They sat in silence. The waves whispered stories too old to be remembered, too sacred to be told.

Finally, Vaani stood.

"I need to breathe," she said.

He didn't reach for her hand.

He just nodded.

"Then breathe. I'll be here. Or not. But you'll find what you need. I believe that."

And for the first time, it didn't feel like an ending.

Just another page.

Half-written. Waiting.

What the Night Unfolds

The city wore a quieter hue that night.

The rain had stopped, but its scent clung to the wind like old memories refusing to be forgotten. Puddles shimmered beneath the streetlamps. Car horns, once constant, now came sparingly, as if even the traffic had given itself permission to rest.

Vaani stood in front of Aakash's door, her breath suspended somewhere between hesitation and inevitability. She hadn't meant to come—not really. Her body had moved ahead of her thoughts, her feet tracing familiar pavements as if called by an echo. The kind of echo that only exists between two people who have never quite finished their story.

The door opened before she could knock.

Aakash stood there, barefoot, a plain grey t-shirt, slightly clinging to his frame from the humidity. His eyes were unreadable, somewhere between surprise and recognition.

"I was hoping it'd be you," he said, his voice carrying the weariness of waiting and the softness of still believing.

Vaani exhaled slowly. "I didn't plan on coming," she admitted. "But I couldn't stay away."

His lips quirked, just slightly. "Then don't."

She stepped inside. The door closed behind her with a quiet click that sounded like forgiveness.

The room was dim, aglow with the gentle light of a bedside lamp. A soft instrumental played in the background—piano notes rippling through the silence like breath. Rain tapped lightly against the windows, as if it, too, was waiting.

They didn't speak at first. They just sat. First apart. Then close. Then closer.

Aakash's hand found hers. She didn't resist. She turned her palm, let his fingers lace through hers. Her pulse quickened, but not from fear.

"I still remember how it felt," she whispered. "You and me. Before everything got... complicated."

He nodded, looking down at their intertwined hands. "Me too. Every detail. It's like my body didn't forget, even when my mind tried to."

Vaani rested her head against his shoulder, breathing in the scent of him—still faintly the same mix of cedar and clove. Familiar. Devastatingly so.

"You still feel like home," she murmured.

He tilted his head to rest lightly against hers. "I've tried to forget how you feel in my arms. I failed every time."

She looked up at him then, her eyes searching. "I don't want to think tonight. I just want to feel. Is that okay?"

He didn't answer with words. He brushed his lips against her temple, so gently it felt like a memory. Then nodded.

"Always."

Their kiss began quietly—tentative, like a secret spoken aloud for the first time. But it deepened quickly, charged by longing and all the words they hadn't said. Her hands slid up his chest, around his neck. His arms enveloped her like they'd been waiting.

Clothes fell away in silence. Fingers traced the familiar and the forgotten. They moved together like a poem being rewritten—every line familiar, but heavier now with knowing. Theirs wasn't just passion—it was remembrance. Reverence. The ache of something broken returning to itself.

When they finally collapsed together, limbs tangled beneath the blanket, her cheek rested over his heart.

"I don't know what this means," she said, voice barely above a whisper.

"Me neither," he replied, brushing her arm with his thumb. "But it felt real. It always does with you."

She turned to face him. "So what do we do now?"

He smiled faintly. "We wake up. And see if the morning still wants what the night remembered."

Morning came, quiet and golden. The city had wiped its face clean. Sunshine poured through the windows, scattering light over the wooden floor like scattered petals.

Vaani stirred, stretching into the warmth of the sheets, only to find the space beside her empty.

But from the kitchen came the comforting sound of a kettle whistling.

She sat up slowly, wrapping the blanket around her, and padded barefoot into the next room.

Aakash stood at the stove, hair tousled, sleeves rolled, humming a tune under his breath. He looked up as she entered.

"Morning," he said, handing her a warm smile and a mug.

She took it, her fingers brushing his. "You remembered."

"Cinnamon and too much sugar," he said. "You think I'd forget?"

She took a sip. Sweet, spicy, familiar. Like everything about him.

"Thank you," she said. "For last night. For... not asking for more than I could give."

Aakash stepped closer. "You gave me more than I thought I'd feel again."

They stood there in the kitchen, warm tea in hand, breathing in each other.

But then her phone buzzed.

She glanced at the screen. Her expression changed almost instantly.

Aakash noticed. "Something wrong?"

She hesitated. "It's from Reyan."

He said nothing.

"He's back in town. He wants to meet," she added. "One last time. For closure."

There was a long silence.

"Will you go?" Aakash asked eventually.

"I think I need to," Vaani replied, her voice quiet. "For him. For me. Maybe even for us."

He nodded, lips pressed into a line.

She reached for his hand. "This doesn't erase anything. It just… needs to happen."

He squeezed her fingers gently.

"Just don't forget how last night felt," he said.

"I couldn't if I tried."

And yet, as the light of morning bathed the room, something about the night began to feel further away.

Not gone.

But no longer untouched.

Because even when love returns, it doesn't come alone. It brings history. And sometimes, the past knocks even when the door is already open.

Chapter Eighteen

The Door That Waited

Vaani agreed to meet Reyan the following evening.

She chose a quiet café tucked behind a bookstore in Fort—one of those timeless little corners of Mumbai where the present doesn't intrude too loudly. The kind of place where every creak of the wooden floors, every steeped cinnamon blend, and every dusty book spine, seemed to invite you to linger in your own silence a little longer.

When she arrived, Reyan was already there. Seated by the window, his eyes traced the movement of the city outside like he was watching a film only he understood. He wore a moss-green shirt rolled up at the elbows, and a pen was tucked behind one ear, like always. A half-finished cappuccino sat in front of him—foam collapsing, untouched.

He looked up when the café bell chimed. Their eyes met, and there was no judgment in his gaze. Only a quiet familiarity. A softness that stung.

"Hey," she said as she sat down across from him.

"Hey," he said, the word carrying the weight of a week they hadn't spoken.

She unwound her scarf slowly, like she needed her hands to do something. "It's been a strange few days."

He nodded. "Stranger when you don't know how to name the silence."

She gave a faint smile. "Have you been waiting long?"

"Not really. Time feels strange here. It's generous. Makes you think you still have some left."

Vaani glanced around. The quiet hum of the café, the old wooden beams overhead, the scent of orange peel tea—it all felt too calm for the storm sitting between them.

"I almost didn't come," she admitted, fingers tightening around the menu she wasn't reading.

"But you did," Reyan replied. "Which means something. Doesn't it?"

She looked down. "It means I couldn't let it end in a message. Not with you."

There was a pause. Reyan exhaled and leaned back.

"I'm not angry, Vaani. I was. Maybe for a day or two. But mostly I was sad. Disappointed."

She met his gaze. "In me?"

"In what I allowed myself to hope for," he said, voice even. "I knew what I was walking into. But somewhere along the way, I thought I could rewrite your story. I thought... maybe I'd get to be the next chapter."

"You deserved to be," she whispered. "You were... everything I thought I needed."

Reyan gave a small, bittersweet smile. "And he's everything you can't let go of."

Her eyes shimmered. "Even when I want to. Even when it hurts. It's like there's this thread... always pulling me back to him."

Reyan reached out, his fingertips brushing hers lightly. "There were moments I thought you were choosing me. Little things—the way you'd laugh, the way your eyes settled on mine. But I guess... love and hope can look dangerously similar when you want them to."

"I didn't lie to you," she said.

"No, you didn't," he agreed. "But not saying something can feel just the same sometimes."

Her lips parted, a protest on the edge, but she swallowed it. "I never meant to hurt you, Reyan."

"I know. That's the hardest part. You didn't mean to. And yet, here we are."

Silence returned, thick but not angry. Just tired.

"You asked me once if he was what I wanted," she said.

He nodded.

"I don't know what the future holds," she said, her voice steady, "but right now, in this moment, yes. He is."

Reyan took a slow sip of his coffee. "Then I hope he chooses you. Fully. Not just in moonlight and metaphors, but in the mess of the everyday."

Vaani blinked hard. "You always knew how to say the exact thing that hurts just enough to be true."

He chuckled. "That's a writer's curse."

They sat there longer than they needed to. Talking about books. About deadlines. About how Vaani still hadn't learned how to eat on time.

"I'll miss this," Reyan said after a while. "You. The way you tug at your sleeve when you're nervous. The way you talk about poetry like it's something you're trying to fall back in love with."

She laughed through a tear. "You noticed that?"

"I noticed everything," he said. "I just hoped I'd matter more in the end."

"You did," she said. "You still do. You will."

When they stood to leave, the sky outside was painted in lavender and rust. Evening in Mumbai had always had a way of making goodbyes feel more cinematic.

They walked to the corner together.

"This is where I turn," Reyan said, stopping near the signal.

She nodded. "I know."

He pulled her into a hug—long, warm, and full of everything they didn't say. When they pulled apart, he smiled.

"Take care of that heart, Vaani. It's full of fire—and it deserves someone who won't fear the burn."

She swallowed the ache in her throat. "And you... keep writing. Someone out there will read your words and see everything I failed to."

"I hope so."

Then he turned and walked away. No dramatic look back. No lingering glance.

Just the sound of footsteps fading into the next chapter.

Vaani stood there for a long while. The wind picked up, gentle but insistent, as if nudging her forward.

She pulled out her phone.

And typed:

I'm done looking back.

She hit send.

To: Aakash.

Chapter Nineteen

The Shape of Something Real

Aakash read the message twice before letting out a breath he hadn't realized he'd been holding.

I'm done looking back.

It was simple. Unembellished. But it landed like a lighthouse in the fog of his thoughts. It didn't promise anything extravagant, but it offered something rare: intention.

He stared at it, blinking once, then again. His fingers hovered above his phone screen as if waiting for permission. He typed and deleted three different replies—one too long, one too raw, one too poetic.

Finally, he sent just two words:

Come over?

Vaani arrived twenty minutes later. She wore a soft grey sweater and loose jeans, hair tied in a hasty bun, strands slipping free around her face. No makeup, no earrings—just her. Honest and quiet and something like tired hope.

When he opened the door, neither of them rushed. There was no dramatic gasp, no romantic line waiting on his tongue. Just a slow breath. A sacred silence.

Aakash stepped aside, and Vaani stepped in like she'd always belonged to the space.

They sat together on the couch, their knees barely brushing. The room held a hush, like it was afraid to interrupt whatever this was becoming again.

"I saw Reyan," Vaani said eventually, her voice soft, but not uncertain.

"I figured."

"I told him everything. About us. That it was always you."

Aakash turned toward her. "And is it?"

"Yes," she said. "Even when I tried to believe otherwise. Even when I told myself it was just comfort or confusion. It's you, Aakash."

He rubbed his palms together nervously. "I'm scared, Vaani. I want to do this right, but I don't know what that means yet. I've never had anything like this—something that feels like it matters more than the music, more than the story I tell myself when I'm alone."

"I'm not asking for certainty," she said. "I'm asking for honesty. Even when it's messy. Especially then."

He reached for her hand and this time, her fingers didn't hesitate. They slid into his like a question already answered.

"I want to build a life with you," he said. "Not just snapshots. Not just milkshake stalls and candlelight. I want the grocery runs and bad moods and ordinary days, too. All of it."

Tears gathered in her lashes. "I want that, Aakash. But we can't run every time something shakes us. We have to be braver than we've ever been."

"I'm tired of running," he said. "Let's stay."

He leaned forward and kissed her forehead—slow and reverent. A kiss that felt less like punctuation and more like a beginning.

They spent the evening wrapped in each other's presence. No rush. No urgency. They cooked a simple dinner—burned the toast, laughed about it, danced barefoot in the kitchen to an old Hindi song playing from Aakash's cracked Bluetooth speaker.

Later, in bed, they didn't make love out of desperation or nostalgia. They didn't need to.

Instead, they lay on their sides, talking about small things. Childhood fears. Embarrassing crushes. Dreams that hadn't changed since they were twelve. He told her about a song he'd written and never sung. She told him about a poem she burned the night after their first fight.

"I used to think love was supposed to be loud," Vaani murmured. "Dramatic. Fireworks and shouting and movie scenes."

Aakash chuckled. "Turns out it's just showing up when you say you will."

She smiled, her fingers tracing slow patterns on his wrist. "And making burnt toast edible with extra butter."

"I'll take notes."

They fell asleep like that—in conversation, in comfort, in closeness.

And in the morning, the sun didn't need to be asked twice. It spilled across the sheets, touching bare shoulders and sleepy smiles.

Vaani blinked awake to find Aakash already watching her, head propped on one hand.

"Creepy," she muttered, stretching.

"Romantic," he corrected.

She laughed and pulled the blanket over her head. "Same thing."

He tugged it back, leaned in, and kissed her cheek.

"I'm still scared," he admitted. "But I think that's okay."

"So am I," she replied. "But I think... we're learning."

And that was enough.

They weren't chasing a perfect ending anymore.

They were building a beginning.

And this time, it was real.

Chapter Twenty

The Letter in the Mailbox

The morning after felt different—not heavy like before, but quiet. Serene. Vaani left Aakash's place with a half-smile still etched on her lips, the kind that lingered like a soft song in the background, echoing even after the lyrics faded.

She walked home slowly, as if trying to stretch time. The city buzzed around her with its usual rhythm—rickshaws honking, vendors calling out deals for fresh fruit, the scent of fried vada-pav wafting from corner stalls. But inside her, everything moved a little slower. The rhythm of her feet did not match the rhythm of her heart.

At her building's entrance, she paused and glanced toward the sky. It was the kind of blue that made you believe in poetry again. And for a second, she smiled at nothing in particular.

Then she opened the mailbox.

A cream-colored envelope sat on top, oddly pristine amid flyers and neighborhood circulars. Her name was printed on it in a crisp serif font—formal, restrained, elegant.

It wasn't handwritten. It wasn't casual.

She turned it over. A thistle crest and the words *University of Edinburgh* blinked back at her.

Her breath hitched.

She tore it open with fumbling fingers.

Inside was a letter. Three paragraphs. Congratulating her on receiving the writing fellowship. Fully funded. Six months in Edinburgh. An international residency she had applied to during one of her loneliest nights, months ago. A haze of heartbreak had guided her fingers to send in the manuscript.

She read it twice.

Then again.

And then sat at the edge of her bed, stunned.

This was the moment. *Her* moment.

But her heart didn't leap. It folded in on itself.

She placed the letter on her desk like it was something fragile and made herself a cup of chai. Then she stood at the window, sipping it in silence, watching two kids across the street fly a red kite.

By evening, Aakash found her.

She wasn't in her room. She wasn't walking. She was sitting on his porch. Her knees drawn up, her fingers wrapped around a ceramic mug, the envelope placed neatly beside her like a confession waiting to be heard.

He didn't say anything as he sat beside her. He simply reached for the envelope and began to read.

His eyes widened. "Vaani… this is incredible."

"I know," she whispered.

"This is—this is what you always dreamed of. The residency, the travel, the time to write. It's everything you used to talk about."

"I know," she repeated.

He looked at her more closely. "So what's wrong? Why do you look like someone just told you your favorite bookstore shut down and replaced it with a mall?"

She laughed—a brief, hollow sound. "Because... maybe the person who wanted this so badly doesn't exist anymore."

His voice softened. "You're scared."

"I'm torn," she corrected.

A pause. A breath.

"I want to go. But I just got you back. We just found each other again. And I'm terrified that leaving now is like setting fire to something that only just learned to breathe."

He took her hand gently. "Do you want to go?"

"I don't know."

"You don't have to decide tonight."

"I want to be the girl who goes. Who leaves for a new city with a suitcase of books and a heart full of courage. But I also want to be the girl who stays. Who learns how to grow without going. Who waters the roots she just replanted."

Aakash nodded slowly. "And maybe you can be both."

She looked at him, tears threatening. "What if I go and we don't survive it?"

"Then we weren't meant to," he said, voice calm. "But if what we have is true, it'll last. Even through time zones. Even through shaky Wi-Fi. Even through pages we write apart."

She gave a small laugh. "I hate how reasonable you're being. I was hoping for a dramatic 'Don't go!' at the gate."

"I've read enough of your stories to know that never works out well."

She leaned her head against his shoulder. "It doesn't. It usually ends in tears and missed flights."

He smiled. "So let's rewrite it."

They sat in silence.

Then he spoke again, his voice lower. "You're not just a chapter in my life, Vaani. You're the ink. The language. The punctuation and the pause."

She blinked hard.

"I'm scared too," he added. "But I'd rather wait six months for you to come back to me than hold you here and watch you resent not going."

"I might miss you like hell."

"You better."

She chuckled. "Promise me something?"

"Anything."

"Write to me. Not just texts. Real letters. Poems, if you want. Songs. Snarky notes."

He grinned. "You'll regret giving me that freedom."

"I hope so."

That night, she sat at her desk with a fresh notebook. She stared at the blank page for a long while. Then she began to write.

Dear Edinburgh,

You arrived quietly. But I think I'm ready to meet you loud.

This isn't a goodbye to what I love. It's a hello to the part of me I still haven't met.

Be kind. She's trying.

—Vaani

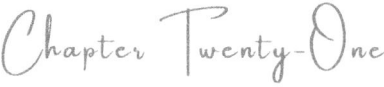

The Last Night

The week slipped by in pieces. Packing lists. Farewell calls. Half-written journal entries she wasn't sure whether to finish or toss. The days were filled with errands, final meetings with professors, and thoughtful glances from classmates who didn't know how to say goodbye without sounding dramatic. But the nights—those endless, quiet hours—wrapped around her like the edge of a poem she didn't know how to end.

On her last evening in Mumbai, Vaani walked slowly across the lane, her shawl draped carelessly over her shoulder. Her chest felt like a page held too tightly, like it might tear if she exhaled too hard. Aakash had left the door ajar, as promised. She didn't knock.

Inside his apartment glowed in amber light. A single lamp in the corner flickered softly. The scent of cinnamon and honey lingered in the air. Two wine glasses stood ready on the floor, and soft jazz played in the background—the same playlist they'd once listened to during their first rain-drenched evening together.

Aakash stood barefoot in the kitchen, in a faded grey tee and track pants, slicing strawberries on a wooden board. He looked up as she entered.

"You remembered," she said, taking off her shawl and setting it gently on the back of the chair.

"I remember everything about you," he said, his voice calm but warm. "Right down to your irrational hatred for pineapples on pizza."

She smiled, walking toward him. "And your equally irrational love for ketchup with literally everything."

He chuckled, setting the knife aside. "Truce, just for tonight?"

"Truce," she whispered.

He opened his arms, and she stepped into them. He held her like she was something sacred, not something slipping through his fingers.

"You smell like burnt sugar," she murmured, pressing her face against his chest.

"Caramelized nostalgia," he replied. "Limited edition. One night only."

Her laugh was muffled by his shirt. "You're ridiculous."

"And you love it."

"I do."

He tilted her chin up and kissed her—gently at first, then deeper, like a sentence he never wanted to finish. Her hands slid beneath his shirt, mapping his spine like she was memorizing the topography of absence. He lifted her easily, her legs wrapping around him, and carried her toward the couch.

Clothes fell in whispers. Her kurta fluttered to the floor. His tee followed. Their jeans tangled at their feet. Skin met skin with familiarity, but not routine. Like music played in a new key.

"You're beautiful," he murmured, his lips trailing from her collarbone to her navel.

"I look like I've been running between packing and crying," she replied breathlessly.

"You look like poetry that finally learned how to exhale."

They moved together with slow intensity, every touch a question, every gasp an answer. It wasn't rushed—it was deliberate. The kind of intimacy that came from being lost and found in the same person.

Her fingers found his jaw as she looked up at him. "This doesn't feel real."

"It's real," he said. "You're here. I'm here. That's all the reality I need tonight."

They fell into silence again, the kind that doesn't beg to be filled. When it was over, their bodies remained wrapped in a tangle of limbs and memory.

Vaani rested her head on his chest, tracing slow, aimless circles.

"I'm going to miss this," she whispered.

"I'll miss the things we haven't done yet," he said. "Like falling asleep reading side by side. Or fighting over takeaway orders."

"Or getting caught in the rain on purpose," she added.

"Or staying in bed all Sunday arguing over who makes the better tea."

"You know I win that one," she teased.

He kissed her forehead. "I'm letting you believe that tonight."

They lay there, the blanket pulled halfway over their naked bodies, the city outside a dull hum.

"I don't want to go," she whispered.

"I don't want you to," he replied.

"But I need to."

"I know."

Silence.

"You'll wait?" she asked softly.

"I'd wait longer than this," he said. "Because what we have—this—isn't ordinary. It's the kind of story people reread."

She laughed, even as tears threatened. "Promise you'll write to me?"

"Every single day. Even the stupid ones. Especially the stupid ones."

"I'll reply. Even if it hurts."

He nodded. "And I'll be here. Same lane. Same music. Same idiot heart."

She kissed him again, softer this time. Like sealing a letter.

Later, as they lay in the afterglow, she turned to him.

"Will we be okay?"

"We've already been through worse," he replied. "This is just a plot twist."

"God, I love your optimism."

"You love me."

She nodded. "I really, really do."

Outside, the city did what cities do—it moved on. The trains rumbled, lovers argued, the chaiwalla on the corner packed up his cart. But inside that flat, under the low lamp glow and the scent of something almost sweet in the air, two people held onto the night.

Time paused.

Memory lingered.

And love, like the wine they forgot to drink, waited patiently on the floor.

Not the end.

Just a comma.

Chapter Twenty-Two

The Departure

The day Vaani left, Mumbai wore its rain like regret. The monsoon had returned not with fury, but with a gentleness that clung to everything. The streets shimmered in grey sheen, auto-rickshaws blurred past in stripes of yellow and black, and puddles held reflections of skies too heavy to speak.

Vaani stood by the gate of her building, suitcase by her side, umbrella in hand, her fingers curled so tightly around the handle that her knuckles were pale. She looked at the taxi's blinking hazard lights like they were counting down the final seconds to a goodbye she still didn't know how to say.

And then he came.

Aakash, breathless, soaked through from head to toe. His shirt clung to his chest, his hair matted to his forehead, water dripping from his chin. But his eyes—those were dry. Wide. Searching.

"You made it," she said softly, unfolding the umbrella and holding it out toward him.

"I almost didn't," he said, stepping into her space. Rainwater trailed down his face, but he didn't wipe it. "I stood in my room staring at the wall, trying to convince myself that letting you go quietly was the right thing. That not showing up would somehow make it easier for both of us."

"And did it?"

He exhaled, a shaky breath. "No. It felt like I was standing in the ruins of something I wasn't ready to walk away from."

They stood there, two silhouettes beneath a black canopy of fabric, rain wrapping around their small island of stillness. The world felt far away.

"I couldn't sleep last night," she said. "I kept folding and unfolding my clothes. I kept wondering what to leave behind and what to carry. And then I realized—no matter how light my bag was, my heart was going to weigh more."

He reached for her free hand and took it in his. "You're allowed to carry both, you know. The ache and the dream."

She looked up, blinking away the water pooling in her lashes. "You're such a writer."

He grinned. "And you're such a storm."

The driver gave a gentle honk—more a whisper than a demand.

"I have to go," she murmured, the umbrella trembling slightly in her grip.

"I know," he said, his voice barely audible.

He pulled something from his jacket pocket. A folded piece of paper, smudged slightly from the rain.

"One more note. For the road. Don't read it now. Save it for when you need to remember."

She took it and tucked it into her jacket without unfolding it. "Will you be okay?"

He smiled, but it didn't reach his eyes. "I'll miss you every time it rains. Every time someone says the word 'almost.' Every time I hear your favorite playlist by accident. But yes. I'll find a way to be okay. Eventually."

"Promise me you won't stop playing. Or writing."

"Promise me you won't shrink yourself to make space for the absence."

"I'll try."

He kissed her forehead gently. Lingering. Memorizing. "You were never temporary, Vaani."

She clutched his shirt for a breath. Then let go.

He held the umbrella for her as she got into the taxi.

The door closed with a quiet finality.

From the back seat, she turned and looked at him.

He didn't wave. He didn't move. He just stood there in the rain, watching the taxi pull away, like someone watching their favorite chapter end mid-sentence.

She didn't cry until the car turned the corner.

Edinburgh met her with fog and stone.

Twelve hours and a world away, the sky wore a different kind of silence.

The flight had been long, dreamless. Not restless—just numb. Somewhere between time zones and terminal gates, she had left behind something weightless yet impossible to carry.

Now, everything looked colder. Not just the weather. The spaces between people. The shadows beneath windows.

It was a beautiful city—but not hers. Not yet.

The buildings were older than memory, streets winding and poetic, wrapped in ivy and echoes. Her apartment overlooked a cobbled square where an old man sold croissants in the morning and books in the afternoon.

On weekdays, she walked past cathedrals veiled in mist, their spires dissolving into low-hanging clouds. The pavements were lined with forgotten stories—blue plaques, worn lampposts, the ghost of footsteps past.

Her university felt distant in a way Mumbai never had. Professors spoke with deliberation. Classrooms smelled of old wood and ink. Everyone seemed certain of their place—except her.

She missed the chaos. The chai stalls and shouting vendors. The laughter that bloomed without warning.

Here, the silence was softer, but also colder. Edinburgh offered her peace—but withheld its warmth.

She tried to let the beauty of it settle in.

She tried to bury herself in seminars, in readings, in conversations about structure and metaphor.

But at night—

She wrote.

She didn't always know what she was writing. Sometimes poems. Sometimes fragments. Sometimes just a sentence:

"The coffee here doesn't understand me."

"Today, the wind felt like your fingers on my cheek."

"The silence here isn't as kind as yours."

Aakash still showed up—in small, unexpected ways that stitched themselves into her days.

And every few days, her phone would buzz. A message. A song.

Sometimes a voice note where he hummed half-written lyrics and stopped midway with a laugh.

Sometimes just: *"Remember the milkshake stall? I passed it today. Didn't stop."*

Sometimes longer messages—three a.m. confessions about how the nights were too loud without her laughter echoing through the walls.

Back in Mumbai, Aakash had started journaling again.

He played gigs. Slowly. Softly.

He kept her favorite cup on his bookshelf and watered her potted basil plant every morning like it was a promise.

He didn't fill the silence. He just sat in it.

And wrote.

Their love didn't fade with time zones or internet lags.

It just changed. Like music played on a different instrument. Softer. Maybe sadder. But still the same song.

Because some love stories don't vanish with distance.

Some stretch.

Some evolve.

Some wait.

Until one day, the world circles back.

And the letters lead them home.

Chapter Twenty-Three

The Strangers We Almost Loved

Eight months passed.

What once had been letters dripping with longing began thinning into check-ins. The poetry faded. The rhythm slowed. Vaani and Aakash still wrote, but the cadence changed. It became functional—*Are you eating well? Did you perform last night?*—instead of confessional. Instead of aching. Instead of magic.

Calls were shorter. Sometimes missed altogether. 'I'll call you later' turned into 'Let's try tomorrow.'

And then, silence. Not angry. Just... distant.

In Edinburgh, Vaani noticed Jamie.

Jamie, with his tattered denim jacket and fingers perpetually smudged with ink. He ran the poetry club with a calm charm that made everyone feel they were already writers. He quoted Sylvia Plath while sipping black tea and carried a notebook that always had a fresh poem waiting to unfold.

He wasn't dramatic. He didn't try to rescue Vaani from anything. He just listened, quietly, as if every unspoken truth she offered was sacred.

The session that evening had peeled something raw in her. Her classmate had read a poem about losing a parent—grief steeped in metaphor, but Vaani had heard the truth of it in every line. It had stirred something in her chest she hadn't named in months.

When she read next, her own words trembled on the page. A poem about distance. About not knowing when to stop waiting. Her voice cracked halfway through. No one interrupted. Not even Jamie, who simply nodded from the back row—like he understood that some heartbreaks weren't meant to be edited.

After the session, as the others drifted away beneath the Edinburgh drizzle, Jamie offered to walk her back to her flat. It was raining, of course—it always was in Edinburgh. Her umbrella kept flipping in the wind, and her scarf tangled in her hair.

"You've got a storm stuck in your scarf," Jamie said, gently helping untangle it.

"Fits the mood," Vaani replied, chuckling. "I think I'm becoming a cliché."

Jamie smiled. "You've always been poetry, Vaani. Even when you're soaked to the bone."

Outside her door, he paused.

"You're always somewhere else when you smile," he said. "Like your heart's trying to send postcards to a place you haven't lived in for a while."

She hesitated, searching his face. "I suppose I still have a few return addresses open."

"I don't mind the wait," he said. "Just… don't forget to forward the mail."

He leaned in—not quite a kiss. More a question. His lips barely grazed her cheek, warm despite the wind.

"I won't ask for more," he whispered. "But if you ever want to stop being someone else's ghost, I'll be here."

She didn't say anything.

He stepped back. Left her standing in the doorway, the keys cold in her hand, her heart even colder.

Back in Mumbai, Aakash met Tara.

She worked in an art gallery in Kala Ghoda and painted her nails a new color every day. She wore rings on each finger and never walked—she glided. Her laughter was the kind that made you want to find out what was funny, even if it wasn't.

They met during an open mic event. She introduced herself after his set with a drink in one hand and curiosity in her eyes.

"That song," she said. "Was it about someone you lost or someone who left?"

Aakash blinked. "Does it matter?"

Tara smirked. "Only if you're still waiting for them to come back."

He shrugged. "Maybe I am."

That intrigued her more.

They spent time together—not dating, just lingering near the edge of something unnamed. She took him to gallery openings and rooftop parties. He took her to old jazz bars and quiet bookstores. She flirted like she was skipping stones over water. He let them sink.

One night, after walking her home, she turned to him beneath a broken streetlight.

"You're always half here, half somewhere else," she said.

"I don't know how to be anywhere else yet," he replied.

Tara nodded, brushing her lips against his. "That's okay. I've always been good at pretending people are whole."

She kissed him.

It was confident. Certain. The kind of kiss that asked nothing but left the question anyway.

He didn't stop her.

But he didn't kiss her back.

Tara pulled away with a sigh, amused but unsurprised. "Maybe next time, you'll mean it."

He didn't answer.

That week, Vaani didn't write.

Neither did Aakash.

The silences that followed weren't angry. But they weren't tender either. They just were.

In Edinburgh, Vaani curled into the corner of her windowsill with a blanket and a cup of tea Jamie had brewed. It was spiced and too strong, but comforting.

She stared out at the misty cobblestone street and scribbled into her notebook:

"Some people don't fade. They fracture. And the pieces show up in people who offer you new chances when all you want is an old echo."

She didn't finish the thought.

Back in Mumbai, Aakash pulled out the old vinyl Vaani had gifted him. The one with the hand-drawn cover art and a post-it stuck to it that read: *Play this when you forget what stillness feels like.*

He placed the needle down. The first note cracked.

So did something inside him.

He sat on the edge of the bed, staring at the door. Whispering to it like she might walk through it if he said her name aloud.

"Where are you, Vaani?"

But the walls didn't respond.

Just the record player, spinning slowly.

Because sometimes, the distance between two hearts isn't a map.

It's time. Silence. And the fear of calling something broken by its name.

What We Thought We'd Hold

Distance, they once believed, could be out loved. Outwritten. Outwaited.

But time—subtle, unrelenting—had a way of shifting foundations, even those built with the strongest words.

Vaani sat at a café with Jamie again, a week after their quiet moment outside her flat. The place smelled of toasted bagels and pages worn soft with weather. She liked the way the world slowed here—how the rain tapped the window like it had nowhere else to be.

Jamie was reading a poem aloud—someone else's words, not his. His voice was mellow, curling around the vowels with a kind of reverence.

She stirred her coffee slowly, not hearing all of it. Her mind drifted—not back to Aakash exactly, but somewhere in that space between memory and mood. The in-between.

When Jamie finished, he looked up.

"You're still not really here," he said, smiling gently.

"I'm trying to be," she answered, blinking as if surfacing from underwater.

He reached out and brushed her knee beneath the table. Not possessive, not pushing. Just a touch.

"You don't have to pretend," he said. "I like you as you are—even if half of you is elsewhere."

She smiled, this time not out of politeness. "I'm starting to forget the sound of his voice," she whispered. "That scares me more than it should."

Jamie nodded. "You'll remember it again. Just differently. Like a song you once loved but now hum in a different key."

They didn't kiss that day. But he held her hand as they left. And she didn't let go.

Later that night, she wrote Aakash an email. She didn't send it. But it helped to write:

Today, I let someone hold my hand without feeling guilt. I don't know what that means yet. But it didn't feel wrong. Maybe that's the first real step away from you.

In Mumbai, Aakash stood beneath the same streetlight where Tara had kissed him. She wasn't with him now. She had gone inside without saying goodnight.

He stared up at the weak glow, his breath fogging lightly in the monsoon night.

Tara wasn't Vaani. She wasn't trying to be. She was bright and immediate, like firecrackers on Diwali. She laughed freely, never asked too many questions, and never asked about the songs he didn't sing.

At a gallery opening, Tara slipped her fingers through his again.

"You're always thinking," she said.

"I'm a writer. It's a curse."

"You're not writing about me, are you?" she teased.

He laughed. "You'd be a dangerous muse."

"Only dangerous if you stay too long."

They clinked wine glasses. But in his chest, Aakash felt a hollow ache. The kind that comes from almosts.

They danced, and she pulled him close. "You're getting better at being present," she whispered.

"I'm learning," he said.

"Still haunted?"

"Every now and then."

"You'll get there," she said.

That night, he opened his inbox. Vaani's last message sat unread for two days.

He clicked it open:

Missed Mumbai's rain today. Missed you too. A little.

His fingers hovered over the keyboard.

Aakash: *Played your favorite song today. Could almost hear your laugh.*

He didn't hit send.

He just stared.

In Edinburgh, Vaani added a line to her journal:

"There are strangers you almost loved. And lovers who slowly become strangers. I'm not sure which is worse."

They were still writing.

But less.

The long letters had shortened. The prose turned into punctuation. What used to be floods of feeling were now droplets in digital space.

Aakash: *Hope you're eating enough. You forget when you're stressed.*

Vaani: *Thanks. Jamie nags me about that too.*

A beat.

Aakash: *Good. He sounds like he cares.*

Vaani: *He does. But not like you did.*

Silence.

Another day passed.

Jamie handed her a book before class started. "Thought of you. The margins already have my notes. You'll argue with them, I'm sure."

She smiled and took the book. "That's half the fun."

He leaned in, but stopped just short. "Still holding back?"

"Still figuring out if letting go means betrayal," she said.

"You're not betraying anyone," Jamie replied. "You're just learning to breathe again."

And maybe he was right.

Maybe holding on was starting to hurt more than loosening the grip.

They were both still holding the thread.

Just with looser fingers.

And sometimes, that was more painful than letting go.

Letting the Thread Go

It was a late Sunday evening in Edinburgh when the thread finally slipped.

Vaani had just returned from a weekend poetry retreat in the Scottish Highlands with her residency group. Her mind buzzed with lake reflections, late-night metaphors, moss-covered paths, and Jamie's voice as he read verses beneath a birch tree. She had laughed there—genuinely, without the old shadow in her eyes.

The warmth lingered as she unpacked in her small flat, her sweater still carrying the scent of woodsmoke and lavender tea. She put on her kettle, thinking of nothing and everything all at once. It was the first time in weeks she hadn't started a thought with Aakash.

Then her phone buzzed.

Aakash: *Just finished writing a new song. Wish you could hear it first.*

She froze, mug halfway to her lips. The words were familiar. Sweet. Nostalgic. But this time, they didn't tug. They didn't carve her open. They didn't stir that familiar ache in her ribs.

She stared at the screen, thumb hovering. Then slowly, with no anger, no weight—just clarity—she locked her phone and placed it face down on the table.

Not because it hurt.

But because it didn't.

Because she was no longer tethered to the ache.

She had outlived it.

That evening, Jamie knocked gently on her door. "Pub night?" he asked, holding out two scarves and a mischievous grin.

She laughed. "Do I get to pick the playlist again?"

"If you promise to stop judging my dance moves," he quipped.

They strolled through the cobbled lanes, their shoulders brushing, the wind nipping at their cheeks. They passed street musicians playing moody folk songs, and a flower shop that closed too early for the season.

At the pub, she sipped mulled wine and listened to Jamie argue with a professor about Keats versus Plath. She laughed more that night than she had in weeks. Her laughter wasn't loud—it was light. Like something released.

Walking back, Jamie looked at her for a moment longer than usual. "You're different tonight."

"Good different?" she asked.

He nodded. "You're here. Fully. Finally."

She took his hand. "I think... I've been holding onto a story that already ended. I kept rereading it, thinking maybe the ending would change."

Jamie's voice dropped. "And now?"

"I'm writing a new one."

He smiled, lips quirking. "You want help with the first line?"

"No," she said, grinning. "But maybe you can be in Chapter One."

Back in Mumbai, Aakash sat at his keyboard, the song unfinished.

The flat was quiet except for the occasional drip from the balcony where rain had puddled. He had tried playing it again—Vaani's song—but his fingers paused halfway through the chorus.

Every time he sent a message, he did so with a flicker of hope—that maybe she'd respond with something simple. An emoji. A memory. A line of a poem they once quoted together.

This time, there was nothing.

Not that night. Not the next morning. Not even two days later.

He opened her last message again:

Missed you too. A little.

He had read it a hundred times. Had tried to decipher if "a little" was Vaani's way of holding on. But now, he understood—it was her way of beginning to let go.

He closed his eyes and leaned back.

In his mind, he could still hear her laugh from that evening at the promenade. Still see her eyes light up at the milkshake stall. But now, those memories no longer pulsed with urgency. They lived in the past, where they belonged.

That night, he walked along Marine Drive alone. The sea was wild and moonlit, crashing against the rocks with unrepentant rhythm. The skyline shimmered—unchanged, yet unfamiliar.

He whispered into the wind, "Goodbye."

It wasn't bitter. It wasn't dramatic.

Just soft. Full of love, and full of letting go.

Because sometimes, love doesn't end in anger.

Sometimes, it fades—not for lack of feeling, but for the quiet truth that two people grew in different directions.

What once connected them—poetry, playlists, shared silences—became echoes, not anchors.

There was no fight. No betrayal. Just the slow, silent drift of hearts learning to beat differently.

And the hardest part isn't when someone walks away.

It's when you realize you've both already left—long before the goodbye was said.

Chapter Twenty-Six

The Versions We Become

A month passed.

Not a single message between them. Not even a like, a nudge, or an emoji. The thread had dissolved—not torn, not snapped—but slipped quietly through two open palms. What remained were the memories, the instincts, the way certain songs still made Vaani glance toward her phone without realizing.

In Edinburgh, the cold had settled in. Frost etched delicate patterns on her windows, and the wind outside now sounded less like longing and more like routine. Vaani wore thicker sweaters, talked more in class, wrote more often without the need to bleed into the pages. Her poems no longer ended with "him." They didn't begin with him either.

Jamie had become more than a flicker. He was a habit. A comfort. A presence.

They moved like people who had no ghosts between them. His laughter was louder now when they watched bad movies curled up on her couch. He hummed while brushing his teeth, and she found herself pausing in the hallway just to hear it.

One night, they stood in the kitchen after dinner, Jamie stirring pasta while Vaani leaned against the counter with a glass of wine.

"You're quieter today," he said, not accusing—just noticing.

Vaani smiled. "It's a good quiet. The kind where I'm just… here."

Jamie set the spoon down, drying his hands. He moved closer, brushed her hair back behind her ear. "You're always here with me. But sometimes it feels like there's a room in your mind I can't quite enter."

She hesitated, then reached for his hand. "There was a time when I lived in that room. But lately, I just visit it. Less and less."

He nodded. "Good. Because I like the girl who cooks badly and still thinks she can win an argument about Eliot versus Plath."

She laughed and kissed him.

Later, she found herself curled in bed next to him, her fingers resting on his chest.

"I didn't think I'd ever feel this okay again," she whispered.

Jamie pressed a kiss to her forehead. "We're all allowed a second draft, Vaani. Maybe this one reads better."

In Mumbai, Aakash had learned the quiet art of staying out late. He went to rooftop sets, said yes to recording sessions he would have once postponed, and let people call him back into the world. Tara was a force he didn't understand but somehow appreciated.

She was everything Vaani wasn't.

Wild. Fast. Brilliant in her unpredictability.

They flirted like firecrackers, fought like siblings, kissed like strangers and friends at the same time.

One night, after a rooftop gig in Bandra, Tara had pulled him by the hand to the edge of the terrace. The skyline shimmered, the city humming beneath their feet.

"Still writing songs about her?" she asked, blunt as ever.

He sipped from the bottle she handed him. "Sometimes. Only when I hear wind chimes."

She raised an eyebrow. "Poetic. Still hopeless."

He laughed. "You like hopeless."

"I like real," she corrected.

Later, in the backseat of her car, she climbed into his lap, kissed him slow, then deep. Her hands tugged at his shirt, lips brushing along his collarbone.

"You still think about her?" she asked again, this time with a hand pressed over his chest.

"Only when it rains," he said.

She paused, then smiled. "Then pray for sunshine."

That night, their intimacy wasn't about erasure. It wasn't even about memory.

It was two people touching each other because touch was all they had to offer.

Afterward, Tara lit a cigarette, her legs across his lap.

"You don't love me," she said, not a trace of bitterness in her voice.

"I know."

She took a drag. "But you're not pretending anymore. That's something."

He looked at her, then past her, then up at the same sky he had stared at with Vaani once.

"It's the only thing."

They sat in silence for a while. No jazz music, no metaphors—just the rawness of two people who had once been broken and were now, oddly, surviving.

In those quiet nights that followed—in Edinburgh fog and Mumbai moonlight—both of them found themselves lying awake sometimes. Not aching, but thinking. Remembering.

A laugh. A bench. A kiss that tasted like cinnamon. A song never finished.

They didn't wish things had ended differently.

They didn't want to go back.

But sometimes, when the wine was gone and the house fell silent and the person beside them breathed a rhythm not their own, they thought—

So, this is who I am now.

So, this is who I loved once.

And they smiled.

Because some people don't break you.

They just leave a version of you behind.

And you carry that version—quietly, faithfully—even as you become someone else entirely.

They never had a fight to mark the end. No betrayal to anchor their grief. What unraveled between them wasn't a failure—it was time, quietly redrawing the outlines of who they were.

And maybe that's what love sometimes is.

Not a forever.

But a season.

A soft chapter.

A version of you that had to be lived… so you could become who you are now.

No endings. Just evolutions.

The Crossing

It had been nearly five months.

The seasons had changed in both cities. Edinburgh had begun to thaw from its coldest days, revealing glimpses of sun-soaked cobblestones and blooming windowsills. In Mumbai, the heat had returned with a vengeance, wrapping the city in a haze of dust, sweat, and the smell of mangoes. Everything felt cyclical—transient. Except for the silence that still occasionally echoed in the corners of their respective minds.

They weren't thinking about each other anymore. Not consciously, at least.

Vaani had accompanied Jamie to a writers' summit in Florence—a last-minute invitation, a spontaneous yes, an instinctual escape. They'd shared a train cabin that smelled of citrus and paperbacks, exchanging observations through lazy glances and half-finished jokes. It wasn't love. It wasn't permanence. But it was companionship. Jamie wasn't the person who broke her open; he was the one who reminded her how to be full again.

Aakash had flown to Milan with his band, invited to perform at a fusion arts festival that brought together sound, sculpture, and poetry under the same skylight. He hadn't expected anything from the trip. Not spiritually. Not emotionally. Just music. Just escape. The kind of chaos that didn't ask questions. The kind that didn't require answers.

And then, on a Friday afternoon, in a museum courtyard strung with fairy lights and murmurs in languages neither of them spoke fluently, they saw each other.

It wasn't cinematic. There was no gasp, no slow-motion moment. Just two people, frozen mid-step, holding paper cups of espresso, surrounded by strangers—and suddenly, by everything they hadn't said.

Vaani saw him first. Her breath caught not from shock, but recognition. Like an old line of poetry resurfacing without warning.

Aakash blinked, adjusted the strap of his guitar case, and then chuckled. "Of all places," he said, voice quieter than she remembered, but no less familiar.

She smiled—cautiously, with the kind of gentleness one reserves for a memory too precious to touch. "You still have terrible timing."

He stepped forward, leaving a pause between them. "You still look like the last page I forgot to read."

She rolled her eyes, half-laughing. "Still trying too hard, I see."

"Only with you," he said.

They stood that way, letting the noise of the crowd move around them like waves against anchored ships. For a second, the years fell away. For a second, they were just Vaani and Aakash.

Jamie appeared behind Vaani, holding a program in one hand and a puzzled expression. "Everything alright?" he asked, placing a gentle hand on her lower back.

She hesitated, her gaze lingering on Aakash. "Yeah," she said slowly, "Just... history."

Tara wasn't far behind Aakash, her heels clicking softly against the stone floor. She wrapped her hand around his arm and looked between the two of them. "Friend of yours?" she asked, curiosity arched across her brow.

Aakash nodded, slower this time. "Something like that."

There was no confrontation. No dramatic unraveling. No high-pitched exchanges or cutting accusations. Just four people, each trying to make sense of their own versions of the past while they stood in the present.

Jamie offered his hand to Aakash. "Jamie," he said kindly.

Aakash shook it. "Aakash."

Tara gave Vaani a nod. "Tara. And you must be the Vaani I've heard... some songs about."

Vaani's eyebrows rose slightly. "I hope they came with a disclaimer."

Tara laughed. "Only that they were unfinished."

For a long, awkward second, no one spoke. The air wasn't cold, but it trembled with unsaid things.

"Well," Jamie said finally, "Florence is full of surprises, huh?"

Vaani smiled, this time with sincerity. "Apparently."

Eventually, they walked separate ways. But not before Aakash looked back once. And saw Vaani already looking.

She didn't smile this time. Neither did he.

But there was something in their eyes that hadn't aged. Something that didn't need words.

No promises were made. No regrets voiced.

Because some crossings aren't about reunion. They're about recognition.

The kind that says: *We were.* And now, we are... something else entirely.

Chapter Twenty-Eight

The Lingering

That night, Vaani lay beside Jamie in their hotel room in Florence, the remnants of laughter and wine still hanging in the air. The air was thick with the scent of red wine, citrus soap, and shared stories that trailed off into kisses. The window was slightly ajar, letting in a breeze laced with jasmine and distant music—some street musician plucking something sweet beneath a lantern.

Jamie's hand rested gently on her hip, his breathing even, his face slack with the kind of sleep that comes only from contentment.

But Vaani's eyes were open.

She stared at the ceiling fan spinning slowly above, the pattern of its motion hypnotic, lulling but not soothing. Her mind wasn't here—not entirely. She wasn't restless. Just... elsewhere. Her fingers twitched slightly beneath the blanket, remembering another kind of silence. One with less comfort but more depth.

Aakash's face lingered in her thoughts—not sharply, not with pain, but with the soft ache of something unfinished. The moment in the museum courtyard kept replaying: his chuckle, her half-smile, the way their names sounded like sighs in someone else's story. The way Tara's hand rested lightly on his chest, like punctuation to a sentence Vaani hadn't finished writing.

Not because she missed him. But because she finally understood that you could carry someone without clutching them. That you could walk forward while still remembering how it felt to stand still beside them.

Quietly, she slipped out of the bed, careful not to wake Jamie. Her bare feet padded across the floor to the balcony, and she stepped outside into the cool night air. Florence shimmered beneath her, all lanterns and whispers and cobblestone secrets. The moon bathed the terracotta rooftops in silver, casting the city in a forgiving light.

She pulled her notebook from the side table and scribbled, slowly, deliberately:

Some people don't leave, even when they're gone.

She paused. Let the ink dry. Then added:

And maybe they're not meant to.

Then she stared at the page. Her own handwriting looked like it belonged to someone older, wiser, more tired. Maybe she was all three now.

Across the city, in a modest apartment on the edge of Milan, Aakash sat on the edge of a bed that didn't feel like his. Tara stirred beside him, tangled in sheets and dreams he wasn't part of.

He held his guitar in his lap, fingers hovering above the strings. But the melody that usually came to him so easily stayed hidden. All he could hear was the echo of Florence—the look in Vaani's eyes, the rise of her brow, the calm in her voice when she said, "Just... history."

He hadn't expected the ache. Not after everything. Not after Tara.

But some people don't show up in your life to stay. They show up to awaken. To undo. To remind.

He picked up a pen and scribbled in his own journal:

She isn't a chapter I'm still reading. She's the part I underline, even after I've turned the page.

He closed the notebook, exhaled, and looked out the window.

It was strange—how two people could be in the same country, under the same moonlight, and still feel like different time zones.

Back in the hotel room, Vaani climbed back into bed. Jamie shifted, half-asleep, and reached for her instinctively.

"You okay?" he mumbled, his voice heavy with sleep.

"Yeah," she whispered, curling into his warmth. "Just needed some air."

He kissed her shoulder, already drifting off again. "You smell like the sky."

Vaani smiled softly, eyes closing, her fingers resting against his chest like punctuation.

And across the invisible string of memory that once connected her to Aakash, a quiet acknowledgment passed like static in the dark.

They weren't each other's anymore. But they weren't strangers either.

They were just... lingering.

Somewhere in the middle of what was and what would never quite be again.

Chapter Twenty-Nine

All That Followed

Years passed like the slow unfolding of a poem—line by line, stanza by stanza—its meaning deepening only in hindsight.

Vaani's success came gently, not like a trumpet's call but a violin's whisper—persistent, melodic, and impossible to ignore. Her writing was selected for a global anthology, her words translated into languages she barely understood. She was invited to teach a short-term writing course in Prague, where students jotted her phrases into the margins of their lives. Editors began calling her by first name. Bookstores displayed her novel beside weathered classics.

And yet, there were nights she sat before her laptop, the blinking cursor mocking her. The stories came, sure—but they lacked that old ache. That messiness. That fire. Was this what growth meant? Writing without heartbreak? Or merely learning how to disguise it better?

Jamie remained beside her. Steady. Patient. He fit into her world like a bookmark—never the story itself, but always saving the place she was becoming. They traveled, made risotto in tiny kitchens, adopted a cat with lopsided ears. They made love sometimes slowly, sometimes like catching their breath in a foreign city. But it was never the kind that left her trembling. It was warm, safe—like candlelight, not wildfire.

One night, after a reading in Vienna, they returned to their rented apartment, a bottle of red wine uncorked on the table. Jamie wrapped his arms around her from behind, his breath warm against her neck.

"You know you don't have to keep parts of yourself hidden from me," he whispered.

She turned slightly, her cheek grazing his. "What if they're not hidden? Just... somewhere else."

He didn't push. Just kissed her temple and poured them both a drink.

Jamie wanted to talk about their future, sometimes. Kids. Moving back to Edinburgh. A small place by the coast.

"Would you be happy teaching full-time?" he asked once over breakfast.

Vaani stirred her tea. "Maybe. Or maybe I'd just write more in the quiet."

He smiled. "As long as your quiet has space for me."

She kissed his cheek, but her silence said more than she realized.

In Mumbai, Aakash's life no longer looked like the version he had once imagined.

The band struggled—two bookings cancelled, a producer who ghosted them, studio time lost to excuses. His lyrics, once born from longing, now felt like rehearsals. Tara told him he was distracted. He said he was tired.

They argued over stupid things. Laundry. Dishes. Silence. One night, after fighting about how he hadn't shown up at her gallery opening, Tara slammed a glass down on the counter.

"You're still haunted by someone who's not even a ghost anymore," she said.

He looked at her, empty. "She's not haunting me. She's part of me."

That night, they had sex like it was a war. Their hands fought for dominance, their mouths swallowed apology and anger in equal measure. Clothes were ripped, buttons popped. She bit his shoulder hard enough to bruise.

After, Tara lay naked on the floor, cigarette burning between her fingers. Her back arched against the cool tiles.

"You were thinking about her," she said. It wasn't a question.

Aakash sat beside her, legs stretched out, a bottle of beer pressed against his lips.

He didn't answer.

"She's gone, Aakash. She's building her life somewhere else. You should too."

He looked down. "I don't want her back," he said finally. "I just don't know how to be someone else."

She took a drag, exhaled. "Then stop trying. Be this version. Be broken. Be messy. But be honest."

Neither of them said much after that. But it was the first real thing either of them had said in weeks.

Back in Prague, Vaani stared at a photograph Jamie had taken of her while she was reading at a café—sunlight on her shoulder, her mouth mid-sentence, eyes lost in thought.

He had titled it "The Version You Don't Share."

She traced the curve of her smile in the image and wondered: who was she now? Who had she been?

Because time doesn't erase. It layers. It rewrites without deleting.

At her next book reading, someone asked during the Q&A, "Do you believe in one great love?"

She hesitated before replying. "I believe in many versions of love. Some stay. Some shape you and go. But each teaches you something about how much space your heart can hold."

And Aakash? He picked up his guitar less and less. But when he did, the melodies had changed. Softer. Less about loss, more about memory.

He no longer wrote about Vaani. But he sometimes sang like he still missed her.

Not the woman she became. But the boy he was when he loved her.

The versions of themselves they had discovered in each other... still lived somewhere.

Quiet.

Unspoken.

Carried gently through the noise of all that followed.

Chapter Thirty

The Storm We Didn't See Coming

The call came like thunder on a windless night—unnatural, jarring, and too sudden to process.

Vaani was in a hotel room in Prague, her suitcase half-packed, the city's dusky silence pressing against the windows. It was 3:17 AM. She was up late, not from restlessness, but reflection. She had just completed her residency. Her room was littered with annotated manuscripts, poetry drafts, and wine-soaked gratitude cards from students.

The phone buzzed. A Mumbai number. She stared at it for too long.

"Hello?" Her voice came out small, half-swallowed.

"Is this Vaani Kapoor?"

"Yes," she said, slowly.

"I'm Aakash's brother. Sorry to call so late. There's been an accident."

Her heart didn't drop. It seized.

"What happened?" she breathed.

"Late night ride. A scooter. A drunk driver ran a red light. He's okay, Vaani. Conscious. Stable. A fractured leg. Some minor head trauma."

Her knees gave out, and she sat on the edge of the bed like the floor had disappeared.

"I thought you should know," he said gently. "You were... important to him."

Were.

She didn't cry. But something inside her—a quiet tether—snapped.

By 5:00 AM, she had changed her flight.

The hospital was cold in that unkind, clinical way. Too many things beeped. Too many strangers moved without looking you in the eye.

Room 413.

She pushed the door open gently.

Aakash lay in bed, pale and bandaged, IV in his arm, cast on his leg, bruises peeking through his hospital gown. His eyes opened slowly. And then widened.

"Vaani?" he croaked.

She dropped her bag by the chair and walked toward him. "Hi," she whispered.

"You came," he said, disbelieving. "You actually came."

"Of course I did," she said, brushing her windblown hair behind her ear. "Even if we're not us anymore. Even if it's complicated. I still care."

He looked at her like a man watching a ghost who decided to stay.

"I didn't think you'd still feel anything," he said.

"I didn't think I did either. But apparently my heart never got the memo."

He chuckled, then winced. "Ow. Laughing hurts."

"Then stop being poetic and dramatic," she scolded lightly.

"I thought I was dying," he admitted. "There was this moment—just before I blacked out—and all I could think was, I never said goodbye to her properly."

She sat beside him, taking his hand carefully.

"I'm here now."

Silence.

"I saw your interview last month," he said. "You spoke about rediscovering your voice. About how sometimes, love just teaches us how to leave."

"It did."

"Did it make you bitter?"

"No," she said. "It made me brave."

He looked away. "I was afraid this would happen. That I'd lose you to something you found in yourself."

She exhaled. "That's not what you lost me to. You lost me to hesitation. To silence. To the version of you that couldn't say what you felt until it was too late."

Aakash looked at her then, eyes shining. "And yet, here you are."

"I'm not here for a fairytale ending," she said gently. "I'm here because love doesn't vanish. It just... shifts."

He swallowed hard. "Tara left. She couldn't handle the fact that I still think in metaphors that sound like you."

"I'm sorry," Vaani said.

"I'm not. Maybe this had to happen. Maybe the crash was just the thing that made me stop crashing into myself."

She touched his hand again. "I needed to see that you were okay. And I needed to see that I'm okay without you."

He smiled through the ache. "That's the cruelest kindness you've ever given me."

She laughed. A broken, real sound. "I'll always root for you, Aakash. But I'm not your audience anymore."

He closed his eyes. One tear slipped out. "I'll still write for you."

"I know," she said, standing up. "But now I write for me."

She leaned over, pressed a soft kiss to his forehead, and whispered, "Goodbye, my almost."

As she walked to the door, he opened his eyes one last time.

"Thank you for showing up," he said.

She looked back.

"Thank you for surviving," she said.

And then she was gone.

Outside, Mumbai pulsed under the weight of monsoon skies. Inside, Aakash finally let the tears come.

Not for her.

But for the boy he had been.

The one she had loved.

And for the man he was still trying to become.

Because some storms don't shatter. They sober.

And in their wake, they leave a strange peace.

The kind that says:

You made it.

Now begin again.

The Morning After the Goodbye

The city looked different. Not because of the rain or the air or even the way the waves curled along Marine Drive. It was Vaani who had changed. And change, she'd come to learn, could rewrite everything you thought you recognized.

She walked quietly, the early morning light brushing against her skin, the wind tangling her hair in a familiar knot of salt and softness. Her phone remained buried in her pocket. She didn't need music. The city was enough.

Last night still echoed within her—not as a sharp pain, but as a dull, lasting ache. The kind you don't want to medicate because it reminds you that you loved, and that it mattered.

Closure, she had discovered, wasn't a door slamming shut. It was a window cracked open, letting the past breathe out.

By afternoon, she returned to her childhood home in Colaba. Her mother greeted her with warm arms and spiced chai, the way she always had. The television murmured an old movie in the background, and for a brief moment, Vaani allowed herself to sink into that nostalgia.

She sat in the living room, tracing the rim of her teacup as the steam clouded her glasses. Her mother said nothing, sensing the silence Vaani needed more than words. They didn't speak of hospitals or old lovers or goodbyes. Just the weather. And the perfect crispness of the pakoras.

But her thoughts kept drifting. Back to Room 413. To Aakash, lying still but alive. To his hand in hers, and that almost-smile he gave her when she said goodbye.

His eyes had said something then. Not 'stay.' Not even 'come back.' Just... thank you.

That night, in her old bedroom, Vaani opened her leather-bound journal again. The same one she had abandoned before Prague. She sat by the window, the breeze kissing her cheek, and began to write.

"Some people are not meant to stay. Some just arrive to show you how far you've come."

In his apartment, two weeks after being discharged, Aakash hobbled from the bed to the living room. His cast itched. The silence of the walls was louder now, but it no longer scared him. He poured himself a glass of water and paused in front of the bookshelf.

There, tucked between a record sleeve and a collection of Neruda's poetry, was an old USB drive.

He plugged it in. And found the song—the one he never finished. The one he began on a night when Vaani had fallen asleep on his chest, breathing softly to the rhythm of his heartbeat.

He sat on the edge of his couch and picked up his guitar. The first chords came hesitantly. Then slowly, they flowed.

He didn't over-edit. Didn't try to make it sound polished. He let it stay raw. Fragile. Like him.

He recorded it with the voice notes app on his phone. No filters. Just breath and strings. He titled the file simply: "The Last Verse."

No subject line. No text. He emailed it to one person.

In Prague, Vaani had just returned to her apartment. She slipped off her boots, hung her coat, and checked her inbox. She wasn't expecting anything meaningful.

But there it was. From: Aakash. No message. Just the file.

She stared at it for a long while, then poured herself a glass of wine. She lit a candle. Dimmed the lights. Pulled her blanket around her like armor. And hit play.

His voice filled the room.

It wasn't a love song. Not really. It was a story. Of a boy who couldn't say the right things until it was too late. Of a girl who stayed anyway. Of a silence that made them both louder.

And it was honest. Devastatingly so. There were places where his voice cracked. Where his breath caught. Where her name was whispered like prayer, not memory.

By the time the last note faded, Vaani wasn't crying. She was smiling.

Because the song didn't ask her to come back. It just said: Thank you for coming.

And that, she thought, was the kindest goodbye she'd ever received.

She closed her laptop and walked to the window. Outside, Prague shimmered with snowfall. Inside, her heart felt still.

Not empty. Not undone.

Just… quiet.

Because some endings don't tear you apart. They tuck you in.

And let you rest.

And maybe, just maybe—when the sky speaks back—it does so in the quietest, most beautiful way.

Chapter Thirty-Two

The Last Song

It happened quietly.

No sirens. No alarms. No cinematic build-up or collapsing scene. Just a quiet unraveling. Like the final thread of a once-tight knot slowly coming undone in the dark.

Aakash's body, which had once seemed resilient through the bruises and fractures, began to give way. First came the fatigue—no matter how much he rested, he always seemed tired. Then the nausea. Then the breathlessness. A general disorientation that couldn't be explained by painkillers or late-night worries.

The doctors called it systemic failure. Post-trauma complications. A rare autoimmune trigger. They used language like 'flare-up,' 'regression,' 'unpredictable.' None of it made sense to anyone who loved him.

By the time Vaani got the call, he had already been moved into the ICU.

She was in Prague. It was early. The sky outside was a blank, frost-washed canvas. She was holding a warm mug of tea, standing barefoot by the window when her phone buzzed. Indian number. Unknown.

She answered.

Aakash's brother. His voice—low, cracking. The second sentence split her in two.

"He asked for you."

Everything blurred. The walls. The floor. Her body collapsed into the nearest chair. "What do you mean? What happened?"

"He... he's not doing well, Vaani. He's asking for you. Over and over."

"I'll come," she said, but the words tasted like dust.

The flight. The frantic packing. The hollow ache of airports. She moved through checkpoints and terminals like a ghost, her thoughts flickering between prayer and panic.

But by the time she landed in Mumbai, he was gone.

Rain met her at the gate. The city, heavy with monsoon, wept with her.

The taxi ride was silent. The hospital loomed—grey and sterile. Familiar in all the wrong ways. She walked its halls like someone in a dream.

When Aakash's mother saw her, she didn't speak. She simply embraced her. Their tears did the talking.

"He kept asking if you'd heard it," she murmured, hands trembling.

"Hear what?" Vaani asked, voice barely a whisper.

"He left you something," the mother said, placing a trembling hand on her cheek.

A nurse stepped forward, pressing a small envelope into her hand. Her name, scribbled in his handwriting.

Inside: a pen drive. And a note.

Play it when you can breathe again. Not before. I hope you smile. —A.

That night, Vaani sat cross-legged on the floor of her childhood room, laptop open, candle light flickering against the walls. Rain streaked the windows like ink.

She plugged in the drive.

One file, "Until the Sky Breaks."

She hesitated.

Then clicked.

Soft chords filled the room. Slower than his usual rhythm. The kind of tempo you play when you're tired, but not yet ready to stop.

Then his voice—lower, raspy, almost breaking.

"If love was a door, You were the light behind it. If home had a voice, It echoed when you smiled."

Her eyes welled.

"You never owed me forever, But I still wrote you into every one of my songs. And if you're hearing this, It means I didn't make it to the last verse. But I made it to you."

The next lines came like a gut punch.

"I was never afraid to fall, Only afraid you wouldn't be there when I landed. But you always were. Even when you left. Even now."

Tears streamed down her face. Not loud sobs. Just silent devastation—the kind that clutches your throat and won't let go.

When the last note faded, the silence that followed was almost cruel.

She sat still. Letting grief take the space it needed.

Then she played it again.

And again.

Because sometimes, goodbye isn't a word. It's a melody.

In the days that followed, Vaani moved through the city like a half-open book. She didn't talk much. She didn't need to.

People tried to console her. Friends dropped by. Old neighbors left flowers. But grief, she had learned, was not a communal activity. It was solitary.

Sacred.

She visited the sea one morning before flying back—Marine Drive, where so many of their memories lived. She sat on their favorite bench, pressed her palm against the damp wood, and whispered, "Thank you."

She returned to Prague weeks later. She didn't post updates. She didn't wear black. She taught her classes. Wrote her notes. But her writing—something had changed.

It was less about pain. More about memory.

She didn't write to escape anymore. She wrote to remember.

One afternoon, she found herself staring at a page in her journal.

She wrote: *Some people arrive like poems. Some leave like songs. And some stay—in silence.*

Months later, she stood in front of a packed auditorium. Her final recital.

She walked onto the stage, took a slow breath, and played *Until the Sky Breaks.*

No words. No preface.

Just the song.

When it ended, the room stayed silent. Not from indifference—but reverence. The kind that only grief could teach.

She looked up through the auditorium's glass ceiling. The stars winked above.

She smiled, tears tracing a familiar path down her cheeks.

"I heard it, Aakash," she whispered. "I heard everything."

And somewhere—beyond cities, beyond songs—she believed he heard her too.

Not with ears. With soul.

Some songs are never meant for crowds. Just for the one heart that needed them most.

Chapter Thirty-Three

In the Wake of Silence

Grief didn't come in waves. It came in whispers.

Vaani had once read that pain changes its texture over time. That it begins sharp—cutting through bone and breath—but eventually dulls into a hum under the surface of everything. She now understood that better than she ever wanted to.

The world kept moving. That was the cruel part. Prague's streets still bustled with the same tempo. Her lectures resumed. Her inbox overflowed with edits, deadlines, and polite invitations. But something inside her had quieted. Something once bright had dimmed, not gone out—but different now. Irretrievable.

Grief didn't scream anymore. It sat at the edge of her bed like a shadow. It followed her to the tram. It stared back from café windows and train glass.

Some mornings, she woke up convinced she had heard him. Aakash's laughter drifting from the kitchen. The gentle clatter of his guitar against the wall. Not hallucinations—just memory, bleeding stubbornly into the present.

Some nights, she played his song, *Until the Sky Breaks.*

And cried into her pillow. Not because she hadn't said goodbye. But because she had. And it still wasn't enough.

She kept teaching. She kept showing up. Her students noticed something had shifted. A softness in her voice. A stillness in the way she now spoke about endings. She no longer talked about narrative arcs with certainty. She spoke of what lingers between words. About characters who leave—not for conflict, but because that's what real people do.

Jamie had moved on. Gently. Respectfully. Their paths had diverged the way streams separate at a bend—quietly, without resentment. They still shared coffee sometimes, the occasional laugh. But something in Vaani had folded inward. And Jamie, in his quiet wisdom, didn't chase what wasn't his to reach.

One rainy afternoon, she stood by her apartment window, watching the water blur the rooftops like an unfinished watercolor. The pen drive Aakash had left her still sat in the drawer. She didn't need to open it anymore. She carried every note now. Every breath, every break.

She pulled her journal close. And wrote:

I didn't lose you, Aakash. I lived you. I carry you. You are the echo in every quiet room.

Then she let the silence settle. And this time, she didn't resist it.

In Mumbai, Aakash's song moved like memory. Softly. Reverently.

It spread slowly—passed along through whispered links and late-night playlists. Played at cafés that never quite closed on time. Hummed by people who didn't know the story but felt it anyway. It wasn't viral. It didn't need to be.

Until the Sky Breaks wasn't just a love song. It was a eulogy to presence. A reminder that some love stories aren't meant to be known—they're meant to be felt.

No one asked who he wrote it for. No one had to.

A year after his death, Vaani returned to Colaba.

It was quiet. Softer than she remembered. The familiar corners of her past now felt worn, but not heavy.

She visited his old lane. Stood at the rusted gate of his former home. Touched the locked door as if it still remembered her hand. A single marigold bloomed at the base of the steps—bright, defiant.

She whispered, "You were the story I didn't know I was writing."

Then she walked to the sea.

She had written a letter months ago. A long one. Folded and kept in her wallet. By now, the ink had faded and the paper had gone soft from wear.

She sat on their bench. The bench. And read it aloud.

"Dear Aakash,

I'm still learning how to live in a world where you don't exist. But I'm trying. I smile more now. Not because I've forgotten. But because I remember without collapsing. I see traces of you everywhere—in street music, in quiet train stations, in the way people look just before they say goodbye.

You once said love wasn't about forever—it was about showing up. You showed up in ways I'll never be able to explain. And even now... you still do."

She pressed the letter to her lips. Then tucked it into the tide.

She didn't cry. Not then. Some griefs deserve stillness.

In the years that followed, Vaani wrote her first novel.

Colaba Nights.

It wasn't sold as a memoir. But those who read it knew.

The story of a girl who spilled her tea, and a boy who taught her how to write like her heart depended on it.

Critics called it luminous. Raw. Unforgettable. It ended not in reunion, but with a line that readers underlined again and again:

He didn't stay. But he stayed in me.

At a reading in New York, a girl approached her. Eyes bright, voice trembling. "You wrote it like he's still real."

Vaani smiled gently. "He is. Just... elsewhere."

"Will there be a sequel?" the girl asked.

Vaani looked up, through the glass ceiling, where stars blinked like held-back tears.

She thought of the hospital. The sea. The song.

And said, "Some loves don't end. They just wait."

Then she stepped off the stage.

And somewhere, in the hush of a sleeping world,

a sequel stirred—

quiet, patient,

and inevitable.

~~~~*The End*~~~~

Author Introduction

Shiv Bhowmik grew up in the heart of Colaba, where sea breezes carried stories and quiet lanes whispered poetry. A data analyst by profession, he's spent years translating numbers by day and nurturing words by night. In an effort to honor the stories that once lived only in notebooks and late-night thoughts, he began unearthing his old writings. *Colaba Nights*—the story of Vaani and Aakash—is the first to rise from those pages. It's his most personal, stitched with memory, longing, and the city that raised him. A debut, yes—but also a homecoming.

Acknowledgments

To every reader who's ever loved and let go—this story is for you.

To my parents, for being my quietest cheerleaders and loudest champions.

To the friends who reminded me that not every silence is empty.

To the streets of Mumbai, for becoming more than a setting—

you became a heartbeat.

And finally, to the unfinished songs and almosts in our lives—

thank you for the stories you left behind.

Preface

There are cities you live in, and there are cities that live in you.

Colaba Nights is a love letter to both.

To the monsoons, to midnight walks, to old bookstores and spilled chai.

To the aching beauty of words left unsaid.

This is not just a story about love—it's a story about timing, silence, and memory.

Because sometimes, the love that stays isn't the one that stays beside you—

it's the one that stays within you.

Foreword

When I began writing *Colaba Nights*, I didn't know it would become this personal. I thought I was writing a simple love story. But over time, it became a story of hesitation, healing, and the haunting ache of "almost."

In a world of fast love and faster endings, this is a novel about what lingers.

If you've ever waited at a café hoping someone would show up—or walked away even when you wanted to stay—this story might find you.

I hope it does.

www.ingramcontent.com/pod-product-compliance
Lightning Source LLC
LaVergne TN
LVHW061610070526
838199LV00078B/7231